THIS TIME

∞

BY S.W. ANDERSEN

swandersenwrites.com

ISBN-13: 978-0-9990616-2-6

Co-edited by: Mari Hidalgo & S.W. Andersen
Cover design by: Cindy Bamford

Published by: S.W. Andersen Books
Printed in the United States of America
First Edition – August 2018

MORE NOVELS BY S.W. ANDERSEN

Switchback

Love By Design

Somewhere Between Love and Justice

The Price of Payback

ACKNOWLEDGEMENTS

This book has been a year-long struggle to arrange timelines and mesh past and present in a way that made sense. One of the things that made this book so difficult to write was sorting out the science and metaphysical beliefs. As with many topics, you can find articles on a wide range of views. I strived to use as many facts as possible in all aspects, but in the end, it is a fantastical work of fiction, so certain liberties were taken to achieve the desired outcome.

The story was inspired by the belief that some things transcend time and space. I have always loved the idea that the ones we love follow us from lifetime to lifetime and find us when the time is right. I hope you will come to love this story as much as I do and I hope you enjoy the journey.

I have so many people to thank for making this book possible. They say it takes a village, but as an Indie writer, it often takes a town. I cannot tell you how much your input helped get this story finished. My cover designer, the wonderful and talented, Cindy Bamford, came up with this beautiful cover with very little input from me. I believe it captures the spirit of the book perfectly I am so lucky to have her as a friend and contributor. Thank you.

To Mari, thanks so much for all your time and editing assistance. To the Con Crew, for your continued support and pep talks. To Sam, for always being a great sounding board. To GG, for keeping me on my toes when it comes to loose threads and missing words. To Cathy, for all the feedback. And to Sabrina, for always allowing me to pick your brain over little details and encouraging me to learn more.

Of course, a tremendous thanks to my wife, Dianna, who made me a believer that there is someone for everyone. Thank you for your patience when I kept droning on about how to get this book done. I love you and I hope we can do it all again in the next life.

DEDICATED TO THOSE WHO BELIEVE

LOVE KNOWS NO BOUNDS.

PROLOGUE

Fall 1953

The brisk autumn breeze danced across Abbie's skin, tempting and teasing, begging to be embraced as it had each of the last seventeen years of her life, but the warmth of the body curled up beside her, of the soft hand in hers, was far more alluring. As much as she loved the shift from hot, sluggish summer air to cool, energizing fall, she loved Mary more. Though they both invigorated her, sending prickles of excitement skittering throughout her body, there was no competition. Only one made her heart thump uncontrollably. Only one heated her in places no one else could with a mere touch. And only one left her tongue tied and blushing with a simple glance. Mary.

Abbie prayed for control over time and space so that even God himself would be powerless to move them from their spot. The browning grass beneath the tall sugar maple sitting riverside in the forest was the one place they could be truly free—free of suspicious glances and vicious, backhanded remarks. The whisper of the trees held no judgement and the chatter of wildlife lacked crass innuendos. Loving another woman was "unnatural" they said, but no one had ever felt more right. Not Johnny Jones or Mike Cabot, Abe Davis or Stevie Barnes. Not a single one of the boys Abbie's mother had ever made her date had been the missing piece to her soul. But Mary McGhee? She fit as perfectly as the glass slipper on Cinderella's foot.

Abbie's eyes drifted from the soft curves of Mary's hip to the horizon, taking in the changing color of sky from bright blue to pink and gray as the sun dipped lower. Soon they would return home—back to the reality where they were forbidden to hold hands or share an embrace. That honor had been unceremoniously given to the tall, lanky, socially awkward George Smythe by Mary's father.

Abbie seethed each and every time the boy crossed her path, or her mind. In either case, he encroached upon her happiness. Like at school, where Abbie worked tirelessly to reel in her need to steal a glance at her girl across the classroom. It was an exercise in futility and George would "unknowingly" step between them nine times out of ten as if Mary's father had made the boy his own personal watchdog.

Being denied such a simple pleasure was like Hell on earth. Every time she was thwarted, the ache in Abbie's heart became unfathomable and she wondered how she'd ever make it through the day. Then, Mary would crane her neck around George and smile. And just like that, her strength to power on returned.

Abbie's muscles tightened. A deep breath did nothing to soothe the growing ache in her heart. Her teeth ground together, an uncontrollable reaction to her constant frustration.

If only they could run away...

"There's a whole lotta thinking going on over there," Mary murmured into Abbie's shoulder, finishing with a chuckle as she snuggled in closer.

"Nah, just enjoying the moment," Abbie replied. Her southern roots made itself known in her voice.

Mary pushed up onto her elbow and studied Abbie's lopsided grin. "Liar."

Laughing, Abbie rolled onto her side. She propped herself up in a mirror image. "Never."

"Two times a liar." Mary's head fell back as her own melodic laughter joined Abbie's. "You forget, I know everything about you."

"Is that so?"

Mary nodded. A proud smile strung its way across her lips. "It most certainly is, Abigail Louise Carter," she said, slowly dragging the syllables with a sweet southern drawl.

"So then, tell me, oh great one, what makes you think I'm lying?"

"Well," Mary started, pausing to pull a pine needle from Abbie's shaggy, short blonde hair, "first of all, you were squeezing the life outta me."

Abbie's cheeks took on a rosy red hue. "Sorry." But she wasn't. Not one bit. Mary could never be close enough and anytime she had a chance to indulge herself, she took it.

"Don't be. I love it." Offering a soft smile, Mary continued, "That alone wasn't the giveaway though. Your fingers were busy against my back and your jaw was clenched tighter than Daddy's vise. I'm surprised you didn't break a tooth." Her expression fell from one of adoration to one of concern, bringing a crease to her forehead. "Is everything okay?"

Mary did know her well. Better than herself most of the time. Struck by the moment and Mary's beauty, Abbie leaned forward and pressed a gentle kiss to warm, waiting lips. "Everything's fine, my love," she mumbled, then pulled back to stare into those brown eyes that held her whole world. "I promise."

"Now, that was the truth." Mary surprised her with another quick kiss before sitting upright and pushing her long, curly red hair over her shoulders. "Was that so hard?"

"No." Abbie laughed and once again moved to mirror her, scooting closer until they were face to face, knee to knee. "And I *was* thinking…thinking about you. Like always."

"I like that you're always thinking about me."

The sparkle in Mary's eyes was what Abbie lived for. "Well, seeing as how it's my favorite hobby, we're a perfect match."

"We are." Mary's bright smile fell and she looked away. A dark cloud replaced the sun that had encompassed them. "I wish we could spend the rest of our lives together."

Abbie scooted closer. Slipping two fingers under Mary's chin, she gently pulled her head around until those beautiful dark brown eyes met her bright blue ones. "Me too," Abbie acknowledged in a soft tone. She pushed a smile to the surface, not wanting their dream-like afternoon to be soiled by the heaviness of their reality. "But that would never be enough. I'd want ten lifetimes and then ten more after that. There will only ever be you for me, Mary."

CHAPTER ONE

Atlanta, Georgia - June 30, 2017

Scattered gray clouds converged with a vengeance and dumped their precious cargo onto the landscape with no regard for their actions. *The perfect metaphor for my love life,* Dr. Contessa "Tess" Kenner mused as she stared out the window of the tiny downtown diner. She finished the last of her black coffee as she glanced at the Tag Heuer watch on her left wrist. A chirp from her phone screamed for attention. She ignored its high-pitched plea.

Like the twenty before it, the text message went unread. There was no need to look. It was Amy. Wasn't it bad enough she had to deal with the storm outside? Tess had no desire to battle the one at home brewed from her breaking up via a simple handwritten note on the bedside table—"I'm sorry, but we weren't meant to be." That was the best phrasing Tess had found over the years, learning the hard way that "this isn't working for me" and "you annoy the hell out of me" were sure fire ways to set a woman on the warpath. Cruel, yes, but regardless of how it sounded, it was the honest truth.

She had taken longer than usual to put an end to this relationship and it understandably hurt Amy, but it seemed no one was "meant to be" as far as Tess was concerned. Every woman had simply served as a momentary cerebral distraction, appealing to her limbic system for a bit of carnal fulfillment. Amy had been more than that, but still not enough. Whatever that meant, Tess wasn't sure, but she couldn't pretend any longer. Enough stewing over personal matters, she had a client in fifteen minutes. Rain and ex-girlfriend drama were not valid excuses for tardiness.

Leaving money on the table for her usual order of coffee and a plain turkey sandwich, Tess grabbed her bag and walked to the door. An irritated growl rolled through her chest as fat raindrops fell harder on the passersby outside. Of course, today *would* be the day she had chosen to leave the umbrella at the office. Any local would've known better. Atlanta's steamy summers were never to be trusted.

Tess checked the integrity of the bun she'd meticulously created with her long, dark chocolate brown hair and then reached into her bag in search of anything helpful. Finding only her *Psychology Today* journal to be anything of worth, she opened it wide and pressed its glossy pages firmly to her head, knowing full well it would provide zero protection from the elements. Still, the effort provided some satisfaction. With a deepening frown, the creases of frustration grumbled back at her through her reflection in the window. The mole above her left brow jumped with the agitated twitch of her muscles. With a quick glance left and right, she rushed out the door and into the summer storm.

Shuffling into the crowd, Tess rushed up the hill. Her poor choice of cover withered under the heavy rain, turning to mush within seconds. She made quick work of the first half a block. With three more blocks to go, she pressed faster. Tess cursed the fact she'd chosen an office at the top of the hill, ensuring no matter where she walked, it was always an uphill battle to get back. Usually she enjoyed the exercise, but today it fueled her aggravation as the rain seeped into her favorite navy pant suit and soaked her black and white wingtips. *Of all the days to wear the shoes Amy hated most.*

"Damned karma," she muttered while crossing the street.

Two blocks left.

The unrelenting chirping of Tess's phone beckoned from her bag. "Dammit." With her left hand still clinging to the last vestiges of the ruined journal, she dug around with her right until her cell was firmly within grasp. Glancing down for confirmation, Tess took a deep breath and then answered flatly, "Hello, Amy."

"Is that all I get?" Amy snapped.

"How are you doing?"

"That's a shitty question, Tess."

It really was. Tess sighed heavily. There was no time for the conversation they needed, but she owed Amy closure. Much more, honestly, but letting her vent would have to suffice. "What do you want me to say?"

"After five months, I'd like to think you could break up with me in person instead of treating me like some cheap one-night stand," she spat.

Tess flinched at the bite in Amy's words. She had never intended for her to feel that way, but what was done was done. "You're right. I could have done that better."

"I'll be sure to send you a customer satisfaction survey so you can improve when you dump the next woman stupid enough to fall for you," Amy huffed.

Her frustration overflowed through the cellular air waves and landed heavily on Tess's shoulders. Tess trotted through the crosswalk. There was just one more block to go. "I don't know what you want from me. I was being honest with you."

"Does it matter what I want? You've obviously made your decision."

"I'm sorry, Amy."

"Fuck you, Tess."

The cell went dead and for the umpteenth time that day, a slew of curses spewed from Tess's lips. Her suit was dripping, her hair soaked, and she had a client in five minutes. What else could go wrong? At least she had a vest on over her white dress shirt. The last thing she needed was to give everyone at the office a show.

12:59 p.m. The bright time display on her phone taunted her with her future tardiness. She prided herself on her timeliness. That and her professionalism. Today it appeared she would be zero for two. She slipped her phone back into her bag and set out across the final street between her and salvation.

HONK!

"Watch out lady!"

The sound of screeching tires and screaming voices was much too close for comfort. Tess whipped her head in the direction of the noise, coming face to face with something big, red, and metal.

CRACK!

Intense pain immediately followed the crunching of bones as she sailed backward. The world moved in slow motion. Her limbs flopped uncontrollably like a ragged old dog toy. Helpless to control her destiny, Tess said a quick prayer for mercy, then crashed against the concrete and succumbed to darkness.

CHAPTER TWO

Portland, Oregon - Same Time

The sweet sound of Nora Jones' "Sunrise" robbed the nearly empty room of total silence. Elena Jake leaned against the top of the ladder, using one hand to steady herself as she struggled to put the finishing touches on the large canvas. The abstract piece had taken weeks and was finally close to completion, but it would have to wait. With a heavy sigh, she dropped the brush against the metal tray, rudely interrupting the mellow song with an obnoxious clank. An upward puff of air huffed through her lips tossed wayward bangs of jet black hair from her brow.

"You all right? You seem a bit...off," Derek asked from his own working canvas across the room.

"Yeah, just a headache. I haven't been able to shake it since this morning." She took a deep breath and pushed her shoulder-length locks back with both hands, adding a stretch of her torso at the top, then dragged her fingertips down over the short, faded sides of her head before ending with her face buried in her palms. Elena descended the ladder, swayed, and then teetered to her left, managing to save herself from falling by the sturdiness of a solid wall.

Derek dropped his brush and rushed to her side. Playing the part of a crutch, he draped her arm over his shoulder and ushered her to a nearby chair. "I think that's enough painting today. Stay here while I grab you some water."

"I'm fine, really." Her bare feet curled, digging her toes into the warm concrete floor. Sweaty palms rubbed against the leg of her favorite painting pants—a pair of ripped, baggy blue jeans she'd had since high school.

"Elena…" The parental glare from his soft gray eyes held no room for arguments. "I insist. Stay."

She held her hands up in surrender as another bout of dizziness took the last of her fight. Cradling her head in her hands, she tried to will the pounding and spinning to subside, but no such luck.

Derek returned quickly with a cold bottle of ice water and a wet towel rolled with ice cubes from his cooler. He set the towel around her neck and held out the bottle. "Drink," he ordered.

Elena did as she was told, slumping and allowing the wooden chair to act as a brace as she tipped her head back. The cold liquid did help, so she swallowed four large gulps before coming up for air.

"Have you ever had this before?" He rested his back against the wall and crossed his arms. His blond hair and paint splattered blue overalls contrasted nicely with the stark white of the warehouse wall.

"Only once. It happened a few weeks ago, but it was brief." Another long pull of the cool water combined with the ice around her neck brought her a moment of stillness, but didn't keep her anchored. Her head once again tossed about like a small boat in the rough seas. "Damn. I really wanted to finish this today for the gallery," her eyes drifted closed, "but I think I should go home and lie down."

"Or maybe you should go get checked out?"

"I'm not going to the hospital." Dark brown eyes fluttered open. She fought through her foggy haze and looked Derek square in the eye. "It's probably dehydration. I'm horrible at drinking enough when I'm painting and it's hot in here." She chugged the rest of the bottle and sat still. "When are you going to ditch the man bun? I preferred the lumberjack beard."

"Hardy-har-har. Don't change the subject." Derek crinkled his freshly-shaven baby face and studied her carefully, then took note of their environment. Ventilation in the small old warehouse was definitely lacking. The twenty by thirty room had one small window that was sealed shut, a bathroom, and a front door. The paint fumes alone could knock out a grizzly bear.

He nodded as his mouth curved down into a frown. "It is stuffy. And the fumes are strong. It wasn't noticeable in winter, but the heat keeps it all in. I think I'll get a few fans in here. For now, though..." Derek walked to the front door and propped it open, allowing a breeze to circulate through the room. He returned to her side without a word. They sat in silence for several long minutes.

"Thanks, Derek. I'm feeling much better. I'm going to call it a day."

"You sure?" Doubt replaced concern as his predominant expression as he offered his hand to help her to her feet.

"Mhm." She stood on legs that were sturdier than before and walked to her bag. "See? All good," she confirmed with a grin. The fifteen-minute drive home with windows open to pump more fresh air into her lungs would be perfect. Then, she would eat, drink some more fluids, and take a nap.

Her eyes drifted toward the clock on the wall and widened in shock—12:59 p.m. She'd been painting for five hours? Yes, rest and water were sorely needed.

That was the plan, but as she bent over to retrieve her bag, her world fell black.

∞ ∞ ∞

Derek rushed to her side the moment her knees buckled. "Elena? Elena?" He checked her vitals. Her pulse was weak, but she was otherwise okay. "Dammit," he muttered as he placed the wet towel across her neck. "I knew she wasn't fine." Derek combed his fingers through her hair, then pressed his hand to her cheek. "Elena?" he called again. Receiving no response, he sent a quick text to Marlie and then called the paramedics.

"Nine-one-one, is this an emergency?"

Hearing the woman's voice on the other end brought him some relief. "My friend passed out. She's had a bad headache all day." Derek sat on the hard, concrete floor and placed Elena's head comfortably in his lap. His fingers continued to run through her hair, offering the only comfort he could until help arrived.

"What's your location?"

As he rattled off the address to the warehouse that acted as their artist studio, he couldn't help but fear the worst. His voice trembled every bit as much as his hand holding the phone. Elena had always been strong and steady, rarely even so much as a cold. To see her in such a fragile state was frightening.

"Help is on the way," the operator said. "Is she still unconscious?"

"Where are you?" Elena mumbled to herself, then drifted off again.

Derek's head whipped toward her. "Elena?" He pressed his hand to her cheek once more. Her skin was clammy, but she was still out cold. "Yes, she's still unconscious," he answered. "She mumbled something." He leaned his ear as close as possible from his seated position, but shook his head. "I couldn't understand her."

"It's okay, sir. What's your name?"

"It's Derek."

"Derek, stay with her until they arrive. I'll be here with you. Let me know if there's any change."

"I will. Thank you."

"Don't you hide from me." Elena's voice was firm, annoyed, but her lips held a hint of a smile. Her eyelids fluttered, though they remained closed.

As she fell silent once again, the vastness of his powerlessness gnawed at Derek's insides. All he could do was hold the cool rag on her head and whisper words of encouragement as the siren in the distance grew louder and louder in its approach.

When the paramedics walked through the door, he gently lifted her head so he could get up. He stood aside as they began their assessment. It was all a blur and his worry escalated with every minute of examination.

"Do you know if she's diabetic or has any other medical conditions?" one of the medics asked.

In a daze, Derek muttered, "None that I'm aware of."

Moments later, Marlie stormed through the door, her eyes darting left and right until they fell on Elena's body lying on the ground. "Derek, what happened?" She rushed to his side.

"I don't know. We were painting, she complained of a headache, and then nearly fell over when she got off the ladder. She had some water and said she felt better." His gaze remained fixed on Elena as one of the medics retreated to the truck. "She was going to go home and rest, but passed out instead. She's been talking to herself. Sounds like she's looking for someone. I don't know who." The medic pushed the stretcher through the door, sending Derek's heart into a dizzyingly erratic thump. "Umm…you have any ideas?"

"No." Marlie wrung her hands with nervous energy. "She passed out a few weeks ago at the diner too. We thought it was from her poor eating habits."

"She doesn't take good care of herself," he said with a disappointed shake of his head. "She said she was probably dehydrated, plus the ventilation here sucks."

The paramedics safely secured Elena to the stretcher, then one approached, stripping off her gloves as she walked. The tall, toned brunette's look was unreadable. "We're going to take her in so they can do a full workup. She's in and out. Do either of you know her next of kin?"

Marlie nodded. "I'll let her know. Can I see her before you go?"

"Sure, but make it quick."

With a nod, Marlie and Derek rushed to Elena's side. Marlie took her hand and leaned in to kiss her cheek, then said, "Hey you. We'll be right behind you. It's going to be okay."

Elena's eyes rolled around in her head before a moment of clarity had her locking eyes with a steady gaze. She nodded and licked her lips. "You tell Abbie I'm mad at her for disappearing."

As fast as it had appeared, the haze settled back in. Her eyelids fluttered shut and she fell still.

"I will." Marlie squeezed her arm, then stepped back so they could load Elena into the truck. Worry etched her face as she pulled out her phone and called Elena's grandmother.

"Hello?"

"Hello, Mai. It's Marlie." She glanced at Derek, fighting back tears as she spoke the dreaded words, "You need to come to the hospital. Something's wrong with Elena."

CHAPTER THREE

Atlanta

"Any news, Doctor?"

"I'm afraid not, Evan," Dr. Coleman answered in a soft, yet solemn tone. "Tess is a very lucky lady, but she's suffered severe head trauma, internal bleeding, and several fractures. We've finally got her stable. Now, all we can do is wait."

"Oh my god, Evan!"

All eyes darted to the source of the shrill voice. Taking one look at Tess, a distraught Amy rushed to Evan's side. Wisps of frazzled auburn hair protruded every which way and her face flushed bright red from running. "Thank you for calling me." She looked up at him, then once again cast her gaze down at Tess lying deathly still in bed. "Is she...?"

"She's alive. That's all we know," Evan swallowed hard, "for now." His voice cracked as he finished his statement.

Dr. Coleman nodded. "I have to make my rounds, but I'll be back to check on her before I leave."

Evan peeled his eyes away from Tess's battered body long enough to issue a thank you, then his focus returned to his sister. His gut grew heavier with every passing second as he stared at her lifeless form. Well, there was life there, but how much? They would have to wait to find out.

Once the doctor had left, Amy inhaled a deep breath and stepped forward to apply a gentle touch to Tess's right forearm, one of the few places free from bandages or casts. Her gaze swept head to toe and then back again. A soft sob heaved from her chest. "Oh, Tess. I'm so sorry. But I'm here for you. Me and Evan…we just want you to wake up. Can you do that, honey?"

Nothing.

Amy turned away and allowed her tears to fall. Evan wrapped her into a tight embrace, finding some solace in sharing their overwhelming helplessness and despair. He stared at his sister over Amy's shoulder. Sadly, this wasn't his first rodeo when it came to the trauma ward. Wait and watch, that was all they could do. He would be there for Tess until the end, but he wasn't ready for it to come just yet.

∞ ∞ ∞

Portland

Yet another nurse zipped in and out of Elena's room, stopping only to check the saline solution or her blood pressure. Like little honey bees visiting flowers, they'd flutter over one machine for a moment and then hop over to the next one. Much more of it and she might attempt to write theme music for the busy little workers. It was amusing to watch, except for the fact that she was one of their stops. Being cooped up in the hospital room for several hours was already driving her insane. Sitting still was not in her nature.

Elena's attention turned to the heavy-set older woman sitting beside her with a weary smile. Her round face, high cheek bones, and reddish skin spoke of her Native American bloodline. Long salt and pepper hair still held much of its original black strands. Though wrinkles had settled in, Grandma Mai looked much younger than her sixty-eight years might imply, but her dark brown eyes were tired, sad, as she looked upon Elena quietly.

"I'm okay, Grandma." Elena reached her right hand toward Mai, who eagerly engulfed it with her own two warm, withered ones.

"You gave us quite the scare."

"I'm sorry."

"I know you are," Mai replied, sounding as worn out as she appeared. "I'm just happy they didn't find anything. Dehydration and fatigue, they said." She glanced down at their hands and said, "I feel like I'm failing your parents. I should watch over you better."

"Oh, Mai." The words broke Elena's heart and she acted quickly to relieve Mai of her guilt. "It isn't your fault. I'm an adult. I'm responsible for taking care of myself."

"Then you need to do it. You need to take better care of yourself. But I will always worry."

"I know. I'm sorry," Elena said, giving Mai a reassuring squeeze of the hand. "And I will."

"I always tell her that," Marlie chimed in as she popped through the door with a coffee in each hand. She set one on the table beside Mai, then took a sip of her own. Her face shriveled as the bitter cafeteria-made beverage stung her taste buds.

"Yes, you do," Elena confessed. Her eyes teared up at the recognition of how badly she had scared her family, and herself. "I'll try harder."

"So you keep saying," Marlie grumbled and folded her arms across her chest. She cast a motherly glare at her, then rolled her eyes. "I'm such a coffee snob. This stuff is horrid."

Elena smiled in relief of the topic change as Mai laughed. Marlie did make amazing coffee. She was the reason Elena had quit making her own at home. There was no reason to start each morning disappointed with the one thing that got her going. "That's because you make the best coffee this side of heaven."

"With as much cream as you put in it, I would hardly call it coffee," Marlie quipped with a grin.

"We're just glad you're okay," Grandma Mai soothed, redirecting Elena's attention and refusing to let the subject fall by the wayside. "Derek sends his love too. He was here earlier, but had to get to work. You really scared the bejeezus out of him."

"I bet." The bejeezus had been scared out of her too. She couldn't imagine what it had been like to see her that way. "I'll call him after I get out. How long do I need to stay here?"

"Well, it's already late, so they said they were going to give you more fluids and check on you again in the morning. Hopefully, we can be home by noon."

She groaned. Staying the night sucked. It would be better if she could watch television, but her eyes had been extra sensitive since she'd woken up and couldn't bear to handle the light. Worse yet, she wouldn't have the comfort of her cat curled up on her chest, purring her to sleep. *Shit! Chloe!* "I can't stay. I have to feed Chloe."

"Already done," Marlie said, making no effort to hide how much she had hated feeding the feline. "Even though that cat hates every other person on earth, she did seem concerned that you didn't show up to feed her and actually didn't hiss at me today."

Elena laughed. "Thanks. I'll have a talk with her tomorrow."

Marlie leaned in and took Elena's hand. "Do you remember anything that happened?"

"Just that I had a nasty headache and felt dizzy. I thought it was passing and I wanted to go home, then…nothing. Waking up here. Why?"

"Nothing really, but you kept asking for Abbie. You told me to tell her you were mad at her for disappearing."

She searched her memory, then shook her head lightly as she came up blank on both the name and the moment Marlie had described. "I don't know anyone by that name."

"They say the mind plays wondrous games in the sleep state. You did pass out. It could've been anything...something from TV even," Marlie offered, hoping to ease both their minds.

Elena shrugged, filled with a weird uncertainty, yet a familiarity with the name she couldn't place. "I don't know." She looked to her grandma for help. Mai was usually full of theories of the mystical nature, but she sat silent, seemingly in deep contemplation.

Filling the awkward silence that had fallen between them, Marlie said, "It's okay."

Elena nodded along, a faint smile on her lips. It wasn't okay though. She couldn't say why, but it felt like just the tip of the iceberg.

CHAPTER FOUR

Two and a half Months Earlier

Atlanta - April 19, 2017

BEEP! BEEP! BEEP!

Tess was quick to silence the obnoxious 6:45 a.m. alarm, but a gentle hand caught her wrist before she could roll out of bed, trapping her in the darkness created by four slate gray walls and room darkening curtains. The black hole of a room could be unnerving when she was uncomfortable—like now. Only a sliver of light at the bottom of the curtains allowed some sight, taunting her with a golden pathway to the door that Amy was unwilling to let her travel.

"Where are you going?" Amy rasped, her usually high-pitched voice subdued by sleep.

"To work," Tess whispered and attempted to roll away again. She refused to look at the expression on Amy's face. She'd seen it enough times already.

"I thought you didn't have to be in till ten? I was hoping we could have breakfast together for a change."

The sadness in her voice forced Tess's eyes shut. She squeezed them tight in frustration as she sighed. She didn't want to deal with the truth. It was messy and painful, or it would be for Amy anyway.

Amy was sweet, but Tess didn't want her anymore. Honestly, she never really had, but then, she had never really wanted anyone. Amy's caring nature had enabled her to wriggle her way beyond Tess's one-month limit and despite a few annoying characteristics, they did have some fun. Unfortunately, that fun had come and gone, but Amy's determination to change her into the marrying kind and Tess's cowardliness—or perhaps, her own curiosity at whether or not she could be changed—remained, leaving them locked in an unspoken stalemate.

I really should end this. But rather than throw Amy's life into a tailspin, Tess spared her and relied on what she did best in relationships, she lied…sort of. "My client is at ten, but I can't get the thought out of my head that I'm missing something. It's an unusual case. I want to go over my notes and sort through a few more studies before he comes in."

Amy's fingers unraveled slowly as she rolled away, as if hoping to leave a trace of her pain behind as a reminder. "Okay" was her reply, but clearly it wasn't. The curtness had said it all.

Hoping and praying that Amy would be the strong one and put an end to their relationship had been fruitless. How many times would she let her do this? Shouldn't Amy hate her by now? Hell, she hated herself for being so weak.

Tess stared at Amy's back. She couldn't think about it anymore—about the fact she insisted on driving away the one woman she could possibly care for one day.

Now free to escape, a long breath eased from her chest in relief as she got to her feet and shuffled to the long, black chest of drawers. Like some weird sort of instinct, Tess brushed off her wrist, effectively erasing the lingering sensation of Amy's sadness. A quick glance in the mirror gave her a look at her girlfriend of nearly three months. Under the cover of a white down comforter and long auburn hair, Amy hid her face that was sure to be streaked with tears from light brown eyes that had lost their shine.

Seemed that was Tess's special talent—hurting women. Shaking away the looming thoughts, she returned her focus to the task at hand—a quick getaway. There was a black coffee waiting at the diner while she pondered her current client the way she was most content. Alone.

She grabbed her favorite silver Tag Heuer with a black face, a pair of black and blue argyle socks, and black boxer briefs. Today felt like a black pant suit kind of day. Perhaps even pinstripes. Oh, and black loafers. Although it was spring, so…maybe a bit of color with the blue tie. She did enjoy a good tie on occasion.

In less than twenty minutes, Tess had showered, dressed, pinned her hair up into a tight bun, and delivered the expected goodbye kiss before bounding down the stairs, out the door of her brick two-story John's Creek home, and into her white Volvo S60 sedan.

The Atlanta commute was twice as long this early in the morning, but the solitude was worth every gallon of gas wasted. Sorry Mother Nature, the greenhouse gases emitted while sitting in traffic was a sanity saver. She did do her best to recycle everything though. Hopefully, it helped even the score.

∞ ∞ ∞

Forty-five minutes later, Tess had her long-awaited coffee in hand. She studied the notes she had made during the first session with her new client. As one of the top neuropsychologists in the country, she was often referred the difficult cases and she thrived on trying to solve their puzzle. Unfortunately, many of the clients sent to her, both in private and at the hospital, were a lost cause. They only served to advance research and help further the understanding of the inner workings of the brain, such as tumors and Alzheimer's. But this one had a chance, or so she hoped.

A white male, late thirties, well respected as a successful accountant, unmarried and in no relationship, experiencing post-traumatic hallucinations in the form of a Hispanic female's voice in his head. He had slipped and fallen at the mall, striking his head on the tiled floor. The force resulted in a hematoma that had to be surgically reduced. Two weeks after he received a clean bill of health, he complained of hearing the voice. There was no personal or family history of mental illness or any related symptoms and all imaging had come back unremarkable, leaving his physicians stumped and his life in shambles.

While audible hallucinations were predominantly of the male gender, a female voice or an accent was not uncommon, leading experts to believe them to be a subset of one's inner monologue. However, Rod's case was unique. Those affected usually suffered their hallucinations far more frequently and the one Rod had been experiencing carried on in a standard conversational pattern. In most other cases, the hallucination was directed at them, either talking to them or attempting to persuade them. Sometimes, they could even have conversations with their hallucination.

Not Rod. The woman he heard wasn't talking to him and he had no communication with her. At least he wasn't hearing harmful messages. Not so far anyway. Tess hoped to make the condition manageable so he could regain his life.

A gentle vibe on the table top alerted Tess to her fifteen-minute warning. She closed her notebook and packed it neatly into her bag, then pulled out a ten-dollar bill and set it on the table. As she picked up her phone, she noticed a new message from Amy.

I hope you have a good day. Maybe we could do dinner tonight at Juan's?

The tiny letters in black and white reeked of pleading. Tess could practically see the pain in Amy's eyes as she awaited a reply. Though she was a horrible person for causing it and she wanted so badly to put Amy out of her misery, she had apparently gone soft from Amy's persistent efforts. She was also a sucker for a woman's wishes. Though it was her preference to side step drama in her life, the irony that she was the cause of most of it had not been lost on her.

Possible replies teetered back and forth between her fingertips and the keyboard before she settled on a response. *Thanks. You too. And that sounds good. I'll be home around seven.*

As she pushed send, she rolled her eyes and admonished herself for the thousandth time this month. Her lack of strength to say what she wanted in her personal life was beyond frustrating, especially when it was something she always encouraged her clients to do. She should heed her own advice for once, but right now, there was a client to see.

Shoving her phone into her jacket pocket, Tess leaned back and took a deep breath. Present to her surroundings for the first time since she'd sat down, the clanging of silverware against the ceramic plates caused by eager eaters now filled the room like the tinkling of carnival music.

Tess chuckled to herself. She loved getting lost in her own little world—a world where she reigned supreme, having the strength to search out the toughest of cases and the courage to present new, and sometimes unusual, treatments.

In a single breath, dysfunctional Tess had transformed into Dr. Contessa Kenner. The excitement of the upcoming appointment extinguished all self-loathing as she focused on the task at hand. She gave her waitress a smile, grabbed her bag, and rushed out the door.

CHAPTER FIVE

Tess took one last pass at smoothing out the creases of her black pant suit and looked around her office. Following each and every client she would repeat the same routine—a sort of Zen that calmed her mind and allowed her complete focus. The magazines had been neatly stacked, the couch pillows arranged, and the box of tissues centered on the cherry wood coffee table, but dammit, that photograph of a Pueblo Indian kiva with a great horned owl perched at its entrance insisted on shifting to the right day after day.

"Every day," she muttered as she walked over to the photo. "Why are you so intent on annoying me?" If she didn't know better, she'd swear the owl had a smirk upon its beak. Could owls even smirk?

She cocked her head and pondered the silliness of her line of thought for a brief moment before reaching up and resetting the black and white against the dark gray wall.

Taking a step back, she admired the contrast of black, white, and gray, with the ladder leading up toward the light. Tess had always found it to be symbolic of life. Always look up to the light. Never wallow in the dark. Hope. There was always hope. Even if it didn't come in the form intended, nine times out of ten, something good would be the result. But nothing good ever came if you remained in the darkness that encompassed the bottom rung of the ladder. Her mission had always been to help her clients find the will to climb.

"Doctor Kenner," her assistant's voice chimed through the intercom. "Your next client is here."

Tess reached over a perfectly placed stack of files on her desk and pressed the button to respond. "Thank you. I'll be right there."

One last glance over her shoulder brought a smile to her lips. The picture was still straight. Thirty seconds was a start. She strode across the room, reaching up to test the integrity of the bun in her hair as her mind shifted back into analytical mode. A deep, centering breath was the well-practiced prelude to opening the door and greeting her client.

"How are you today, Rod?"

"Struggling, Doctor Kenner." The tall, lean gentleman ambled slowly through the door. His legs moved slow and heavy, as if the weight of the world rode upon his back.

She nodded and stood aside as she waved him toward the couch. Closing the door behind them, Tess studied his demeanor and noted the apparent weight loss and dark circles under his eyes. He had forgone his usual business suit, instead choosing a pair of torn blue jeans and a vintage Jimi Hendrix T-shirt. Were the rips in the denim intended to represent the way his life had been ripped apart?

Taking a seat herself, she set pen to paper and began detailing their session. "No changes in the voice?"

"None. I've had several dreams that were amazingly vivid. So real, I'd swear I was standing right in them." Rod shook his head and released a heavily burdened breath. "But then, I'd wake up."

"Is there anyone or anyplace familiar in them?"

"No. I mean, it would feel familiar when I was there, but when I'm awake, no."

"Are they bad dreams?"

"No."

"That's good. Have you seen the source of your voice?"

"No. And yesterday she was going on and on about how she wished she could find her other half in life. I tried the techniques you've been showing me to quiet my mind, but she only grew louder, like she refused to be denied."

Tess scribbled more notes, her mind going a million miles a minute as she fought to make sense of the new information. Answers. She needed answers.

"I couldn't get any work done, so I went home and had a few drinks."

"Did that help?"

"Nope. Never does. But I do get to sleep easier. Only now, it's these dreams. I wake up feeling weird and..."

"And?"

"Sad. Does that make sense?"

"It does if the dreams are of things familiar, like you said. Could be there's a part of you longing for the things you dream of. That's when your subconscious takes the time to talk to you. Could it be that you're also wishing you'd find your other half? That you're lonely and this experience has only served to amplify that need in wanting someone to help comfort you?"

"Maybe. I don't know. Sure, I'd love to have someone to share my life with. Who doesn't?"

Tess bristled. The action took her by surprise, hitting a nerve she hadn't acknowledged. She had always been happy alone. She truly had. Relationships had always made her miserable. Was that really so odd? Why were people so desperate to become attached? Of course, she had read every book and knew all the theories. Still-

"But I never felt lonely or desperate for companionship."

Rod's voice cut off her internal therapy session and brought her back to the conversation at hand. It was unlike her to stray while counseling a client. Tess shifted in her chair, regaining her composure. Rod hadn't seemed to notice, but the break in her professionalism was unacceptable to Tess. She leaned forward, elbows on knees, and redirected her full focus to what her client was saying.

"I was the eternal optimist that it would happen when the time was right. I have a good life. Well, I *had* one anyway."

"You're taking steps to get it back. The tests I've run and all of your scans were normal."

"Can I really get it back though?"

"I believe you can. This trauma has changed you, of course, but there are ways to manage it. We just have to find the one that works for you."

"I hope you're right."

Me too. She looked away as she closed her notebook, signaling the end of their appointment.

"So, what's my next step? A friend of mine says I should find a witch doctor." He laughed, but his tone conveyed he had been seriously considering the option.

"I'm afraid I don't know any of those and I have never seen or read any conclusive evidence that the work they did was real." Tess set the notebook on the end table and rose from her chair.

Rod followed her lead, then stood there helpless like a lost puppy awaiting his savior. Tess wanted to be that savior. Unlike many of her other clients, Rod was young and healthy and had so much life to live. She needed to be strong for him, to dig deeper for answers, but she was running out of options.

Despite the dread pooling in her gut, she smiled and said, "I won't tell you not to take up your friend's offer. Hope is one of the most important keys to success. I'm going to go off the beaten path a bit and set you up with a hypnotist. Maybe we can get some more details on these dreams to help us out. I'll ask him to consider some regression therapy as well. In the meantime, continue to use the techniques before bed and see if you can remember to ask her name." Tess extended her hand. "Stay strong, Rod."

He accepted her handshake with a nod and a smile. "I'm trying. Thanks, Doctor Kenner."

She looked on in silence as he said his goodbye to the receptionist. Something with this case wasn't right. Rod's condition defied the many cases she had studied. There was not one single positive finding. The corner of her mouth pulled down and to the left in a half-frown and her lips pursed tight. She marched back to her desk, stopping abruptly when the photo was again slanted to the right.

"Son of a..." Tess shook her head and sighed. She removed the photo from its place and set it on the floor. Its blatant defiance of her wishes was a distraction she couldn't handle right now. She opened her bag and retrieved her cell phone, then fired off a quick text to let Amy know she'd be late.

Thinking twice, she scrolled over and set it to silent. No doubt her girlfriend would be pissed, but that was something she could deal with later. Letting Rod suffer the rest of his life, on the other hand, she refused to give anything less than everything to prevent.

∞ ∞ ∞

Tess strode into Max Lager's and instantly spotted her friends and colleagues, Drs. Natalie Smith and Warren Matthews. After her session with Rod, she couldn't wait for something to take the edge off and her taste buds had been anxious to bathe in a pint of Max black. Chocolate tones in a malt beer combined to give her the best of both worlds. Of course, her stomach bargained for a Bison Poblano burger, but she was meeting Amy for dinner in an hour.

"There she is. You look like hell," Natalie stated matter-of-factly. She looked Tess over from her seat beside Warren. Her bright red, side-swept pixie cut, mocha-colored skin, and hazel eyes had her looking very Rihanna-like.

The woman never did shy away from bluntness. It was as endearing as it was frustrating. "Gee thanks, Nat," Tess grumbled and rolled her eyes. She claimed the chair across from them both, then blew out a haggard breath.

"You know I'm generally judgement free," Warren started, his eyes twinkling as he ironically shot Natalie a judgmental look, "but you do look frazzled, Tess." He leaned forward until his bulging belly hit the table and studied her demeanor. He looked much older than his late thirties, a by-product of poor lifestyle choices, but he was a brilliant psychiatrist and a good man. "Everything all right?"

It was great to have caring friends, but caring friends who were also in the therapy field could be a pain in the ass. Sometimes

Tess just wanted a drink. But since their brains were available for picking, she got straight to the problem plaguing her mind. "It's my client. He hears voices, but not in the traditional sense and I'm a bit stumped. Every test is normal."

"What's so different?"

Tess went on to explain, animatedly going through every intricate detail she could recall, and by the time she left, she had gotten no closer to understanding Rod's condition. At least the Association of Neuropsychology seminar in Kansas City was coming up soon. She was looking forward to chatting up Dr. Albert Greenbaum. If anyone could help her to help Rod, the premiere expert in the field of audible hallucinations had to be it.

As she walked back to her office to retrieve her car, her phone rang. Tess glanced at the screen. She swiped to answer and smiled as she said, "Hello, Evan. To what do I owe a call from my dear baby brother this evening?"

"Very funny, Tess. I'm only one year younger."

"Still younger," she teased.

"Yeah, yeah," he responded with a laugh that ended in an uncomfortable pause. "I'm calling, because...well...I told you I'd call, uh, about...you know, going up to see mom and dad soon."

Tess instantly sobered. "Yeah, umm...okay. We will. I've just, uh, got a lot of work right now. That research paper deadline is coming up."

"Sure. Yeah. Um...I know, but it's been a while, so..."

"We will. I promise. I'll even get the flowers this year." Tess forced a smile.

"I won't hold my breath." A sad chuckle filled the line.

"Evan?"

"Yeah, Tess?"

"Why'd they have to get on that damned, shitty little plane?"

A long moment passed before he answered, "Because that's who they were, Tess. That was the best way to get to the village after that storm. They loved to travel and helping people. Where do you think we got it from?"

Tess pushed a rising sob back down her throat. "I know," she croaked. "I know. I just...I'm still so angry that we lost them like that, even after all these years."

"Me too." He drew a breath and harshly released it into the receiver. "This will be seventeen years," he confirmed. The sound of dead air followed until he cleared his throat and croaked out, "I'll see you soon, then?"

"Mhm."

There was nothing else to say. The line fell silent.

CHAPTER SIX

Portland

"Thanks so much for helping me out today, Elena. A Monday morning is the worst time to have an AWOL employee. People need their cup of joe and a donut to get the week started."

Watching Marlie dash around clearing tables with sweat forming over her graying brows was almost comical. She seemed immune to the fact the morning rush had subsided, leaving only herself, Elena, and one lone customer left in the diner. When she finished wiping her current table, Marlie dried her hands on the towel that always hung over her left shoulder, then she picked up the busser box and moved to the next one.

"No problem. You know I'm always here if you need me. Now..." Elena pried the overflowing box from Marlie's grip and set it on the table. "You need to stop and take a breath." Kicking a chair out with her foot and nudging her friend back with a gentle hand to the shoulder, Elena had to laugh at her frantic expression. She waved around the room to create an awareness of its emptiness. "Relax. We fought the good fight and lived to see another day."

Marlie let out a breath and then laughed along with her. "You're right. What would I ever do without you?"

"Clearly, you'd work yourself into an early grave."

"I've got one foot in it already. I'm gonna be fifty-five next week."

"That's a drop in the bucket. You may have almost twenty on me, but you'll still probably outlive me. Stubborn old mules live forever."

"Elena!"

"You are stubborn, so don't you deny it."

"Never." Her chest puffed with pride. "I am, and proud of it. It's helped make me a successful business owner."

Elena smiled as her friend of fifteen years wiped the wet beads formed from a good morning's work off her brows with her towel. Her amber eyes sparked with mischief and determination. Marlie was so alive, so vibrant.

Elena wanted that too—to feel happy and alive.

"Whatcha thinking about over there?" Marlie asked.

"Nothing." Just random thoughts of life, love, and happiness. The usual, but nothing she cared to discuss. Elena hoped to sidestep Marlie's question with a not so subtle topic change. "I'll clean the coffee makers."

Not taking the bait, Marlie folded her arms and cocked her head to the right as she said, "It was most definitely something. I've known you long enough to tell."

"I was just enjoying the moment."

"Mhm. You're a horrible liar, Elena." A pause filled the air. When it garnered no response, Marlie changed the topic. "Tell you what, Kit should be here soon for her shift, so if you'll clean out the coffee makers, I'll finish up the tables, and I'll make you dinner tonight as a thank you."

"Wait. You've been busting your butt. How about *I* finish bussing and *you* clean the coffee makers? And only if you're making lasagna," Elena bargained with a waggle of her brows and a cheeky grin.

"Oh…all right." Marlie pulled the towel from her shoulder, twirled it around, and then swatted Elena's hip. "Only cause it's you."

"Deal." With a clap of her hands, Elena set to task. In the silence, one question kept repeating in her mind—would she ever get the chance to be that happy?

∞ ∞ ∞

"I saw Tracy the other day." Marlie spoke the words casually as she slipped on her mitts and opened the oven door. Fighting the puff of steam in her face, she stooped over, removed the piping hot dish of homemade lasagna, and then set it on the counter.

Every other day they did this. At least, it felt as if it were that often. Either way, the conversation was getting exhausting. Elena's conscious effort not to roll her eyes failed miserably and she thanked the lasagna gods for commandeering her friend's attention. "Yeah? How is she?" Her tone was intended to express little interest. Maybe this time Marlie would get the message.

"Good. She asked about you," Marlie replied, ignoring the unspoken hint, as usual. She carefully removed the foil from the red-hot baking dish and admired the fruits of her hard labor.

Of course, she did. Tracy had spent more time asking how she was since their break-up than when they were together. She was nice and sweet, but a work-a-holic and Elena had quickly tired of all the cancelled plans and late appearances. Elena thought better of herself than to settle for second in someone's life, even with Tracy throwing the word "love" around as if it were a solve-all to their relationship woes. "What did you tell her?"

"Nothing really," was uttered as Marlie pulled off one mitt and rifled through the kitchen drawers in search of something she apparently couldn't continue without. "I said you were fine."

That about covered it. There was nothing else Elena cared to add. "Your lasagna is always a work of art."

"That girl really loves you. Aha!" Marlie thrust an oversized silver spatula triumphantly into the air, ignoring Elena's desire to drop the subject. "For a minute there, I thought I'd lost it."

Smiling at her friend's exuberance, Elena forced herself back on topic with a tired sigh. She hoped it would be the last time. Her elbows hiked up onto the kitchen island and she propped her chin in the palm of her hands. "What do you want me to say, Marlie?"

"Nothing. I was just stating a fact."

"Yeah well...I don't love her. She was nice. We had a good time, when she wasn't working. But my heart wasn't in it, so you can stop pushing the Tracy agenda." She stared Marlie straight in the eye to emphasize her seriousness.

"Okay, okay." Marlie threw her hands up in surrender, a spatula in one and an oven mitt on the other. "But I worry about you."

"Why? I'm a big girl."

"You are, and a very capable woman, but..." The spatula was set aside and Marlie's full attention fell on Elena. "I worry you'll never find a woman that lives up to the one who haunts your dreams."

There it was, the true reason behind the "Tracy agenda." Concern etched itself deep in every fine detail of Marlie's solemn expression. There was no mistaking the seriousness of her comment.

Elena looked away and then grumbled, "No one is haunting my dreams."

"Perhaps haunting is the wrong word," Marlie conceded. "But you deserve to be happy...in real life."

"Happy," she muttered with a huff. There was that word again. The very question she had pondered that morning had reared its inquisitive head for the second time. So, again she asked herself, could she ever achieve the level of happiness she felt in her dreams?

"Yeah, you know, when someone smiles and you can see it reaches into their very soul. When they look at you, there's a light in their eyes, an energy about them that brightens every room," Marlie elaborated.

"Like you." Elena whispered in awe. "That's you."

"I hope it is. I want it to be me. Even though I lost my Steve, my one, I try every day to be positive, to find my happy and spread it to the people I love. The question is, do you want it to be you?"

Letting her gaze drift out the window to the robin perched on a tree limb, Elena admitted, "I don't think there's anyone who honestly doesn't want to be happy." Marlie made it look so easy, but it wasn't. At least, not for her. Not so far. But why?

"That's the first step, my dear friend. You'll get there. I know there's someone special waiting on you. Those dreams could be your sign of things to come."

"Now you sound like Grandma Mai." Elena rolled her eyes again as she scrunched her face and laughed.

"You've got Chinook blood in you and that's a power in itself. You should look into that." Turning back to the lasagna,

Marlie cut two heaping servings and set each one on a plate. After admiring her work, she reached into a covered bowl and pulled out two slices of garlic bread to go with them.

"Do you seriously believe in that stuff?" Elena had to ask. "I mean come on, dreaming of a woman I've never met for years who keeps me from having a real, lasting relationship? Sounds more like I need to see a shrink."

"So, see a shrink then." Marlie shrugged as she added a side of salad to their meal. "Or, a hypnotist, or a witch, or a support group. Talk to someone, but I'm telling you girl, you've got something special about you and I can't wait to find out what it is."

"Special? I think you mean crazy." She forced an uneasy laugh to deflect that her discomfort had started to become a concern. "But thanks. You really are the best friend a girl could ask for. Not to change the subject, but I'm starving."

Marlie turned and presented her prize placed perfectly on a plate. She set it in front of Elena and smiled proudly when sleeves were eagerly rolled up.

"Oh my...that's just...I'm drooling here." Elena's eyes popped wide and her stomach roared its approval.

"Thank you." Marlie bent at the waist and extended her right hand in a formal bow before taking a seat beside Elena with a plate of her own. She cut her portion in two then watched with eager anticipation for Elena to take her first bite.

Three long puffs of air cooled the huge forkful of lasagna that hovered two inches from Elena's mouth. "After this, I wouldn't object to a helping of that chocolate cream pie you've got stashed in the fridge. Just saying." The long awaited hot, gooey, cheesy goodness was shoveled into Elena's mouth without an ounce of shame—nothing new when it came to Marlie's cooking.

"Saw that, did ya?" Marlie waited until after Elena hummed her approval to take her first bite.

"Yup," she mumbled with a full mouth. A hint of a smile played on her lips as she chewed.

"You never miss chocolate. But since you're *you*, I guess I could share." Her response brought out a smile whose brightness rivaled high noon on a clear summer day. "Wow, I can't wait for the day you smile that brightly for a woman," Marlie remarked with a hefty chuckle.

Elena shoved her playfully. "Stop it. No one could ever take the place of chocolate in my heart."

"We'll see about that."

She forced the smile to remain on her lips as she inhaled another bite. There was one woman that could make chocolate a distant memory—one she was certain would taste every bit as sweet and fill her soul with a hundred times more joy.

If only she were real.

CHAPTER SEVEN

Portland - May 3, 2017

"Elena?"

"Yeah, Marlie?"

"Would you be a dear and take that gentleman's order, please? I've got my hands full and he's been waiting patiently."

"Sure thing."

Elena got up, made her way behind the counter, and approached the old man. He was tall and lanky with long arms and pale skin. His thin, white hair was parted perfectly and swept to the left. Thick black glasses perched on the end of his nose as he read the menu.

"Good morning. Sorry for your wait. What can I get ya?"

He glanced up and smiled, but when his eyes met hers, his smile faltered for the briefest of moments before he stuttered, "I, uh...I..." He looked away and collected himself. "I'll have a...a coffee with one sugar and...a bagel with...lox, toasted, pu...please." The old man continued to avoid her gaze, his hands wringing nervously atop the counter.

"Coming right up." Elena studied him for a moment. His odd behavior and shaky hands stoked her worry that he might be in the midst of a medical emergency. "Are you okay?"

With a feverish nod in reply, she watched him a moment longer before conceding and carrying his order slip back to Marlie.

"Thanks for covering," Marlie said as she expertly folded over a cheese omelet on the griddle.

"No problem," Elena replied with a sigh and poured the cup of coffee. She glanced back over her shoulder to find the old man staring at her with a sort of longing that made her uncomfortable. He seemed to have settled down though, so at least she could table the idea of calling the paramedics...for now.

"Everything okay?" Marlie plated the omelet and added two slices of wheat toast. She slid the plate through the window, which was quickly scooped up to serve by the other waitress, Kit.

"That old man is weird. Is he a regular?"

Marlie stopped what she was doing and took a long hard look. The man noticed and quickly looked away, busying himself with a brochure on the countertop. "Nope. Doesn't look familiar. Weird how?"

"I don't know." Elena resisted the urge the sneak a peek at the awkward customer. "He's all fidgety and keeps staring at me."

"Well, you got some serious curves." Marlie chuckled. "You know how men can be. Age doesn't matter."

"Gross. And no, it's not like that. I can't explain it." Shaking her head, Elena carried the cup of coffee back to the old man and set it down, forcing a smile when he finally looked up at her again. "My name is Elena, if you need anything. Your order will be out in a few."

"Thank you, Elena. I'm uh...sorry about earlier. You reminded me of someone I lost a lifetime ago. Your eyes...they're just like hers." He became lost in a stare once again, then freed himself with a shake of the head. "It caught me off guard."

A sigh of relief rushed from Elena's lungs. It made sense now and it was obviously someone he had cared for deeply. "Someone you loved?" She didn't mean to ask, but the words fell out. "I'm sorry. It's not my business," she was quick to apologize, shocked by her nosiness. Her manners were usually top notch.

"It's all right." He swallowed hard. "It was a long time ago. She was my fiancé, Mary." He pulled out his wallet and flipped it open to a tattered old black and white photo. There he was, his hair dark and styled just as it was now, standing with his arm around a woman. "She died in a car crash the day we were to be wed."

A gasp slipped through Elena's lips at the horrific reveal. Her heart ached for the man. How hard it must have been to have lost his love so soon.

She stared at the woman in the photo, becoming entranced by her face. Though she had never seen her before, there was an uncanny feeling of familiarity. The young woman's smile was wide and bright for anyone content with merely keeping up appearances, but at the corners of her mouth, it met a sad end. The smile didn't carry up her cheeks or emanate from her soul as it should someone in true love—something Elena had learned from Marlie.

Then, there were the eyes. Elena was raised to believe the eyes held all truths and the ones staring back at her, looking so very eerily like her own, told her his love had been unreturned. Somehow, some way, she felt the woman's pain. It burned through her chest and tore at her gut, an ache so deep it made her head spin. She pried her eyes away and steadied herself on the edge of the counter, sucking in a deep breath. "She was beautiful. I'm sorry for your loss."

His gaze remained fixed on the photo, oblivious to Elena's discomfort. "Some things you never get over." The heaviness in his heart carried over to his words. He closed his wallet and shoved it back into his pocket. "But I've had a good life, a loving wife, and a beautiful, healthy daughter. I guess it all worked out the way it was supposed to."

Elena forced a smile and walked away, pushing down the uneasiness wringing her stomach tight like a wet kitchen rag. Unsteady legs carried her back to the kitchen. She grabbed a handful of ice cubes and pressed them to her head as she plopped into a chair. The room took off in a slow spin again.

A flash before her eyes—sitting in a car, careening through a guard rail, and sailing off the edge of a cliff. Fear replaced uneasiness, paralyzingly so. Before she could even question what had happened, nausea set in and then everything went black.

∞ ∞ ∞

Elena awoke to Marlie fanning her with one hand while the other wiped her brow with a cold, wet towel. Kit watched with concern from the corner as she kept an eye on the customers through the serving window.

"Oh, thank heavens. You really gave me a scare. I was about to call the medics. How're you feeling?" Marlie's expression held the tenderness and worry of a mother.

"I'm…okay, I guess." Elena glanced left and right, then settled on Kit, who gave her a smile before leaving. "What happened?"

"I was hoping you could tell me. Did that old man slip you something?"

"Old man?"

"Yeah, the one you said weirded you out?"

It all came roaring back, but what had happened was still a mystery. So vague, yet so extremely personal. She lacked the words to explain. Who would even believe such a thing anyway? Actually, Marlie probably would.

With a shake of her head she said, "No, he didn't. He was fine, actually. I think it's because I skipped breakfast." That reasoning would suffice. For now.

"How many times do I have to tell you to take better care of yourself?" her friend chided with a stern expression and a pointing finger.

"At least once more?" She smiled sheepishly and shrugged. "Sorry. I'll do better. Promise."

"I'm going to hold you to it this time, missy. Now, you stay right there and eat everything on the plate I bring you. Understood?"

"Yes, ma'am." Accepting the glass Marlie handed her, Elena drank the water while a new plate of scrambled eggs, toast, and orange slices was prepared just for her.

"Marlie, is he still here?"

"No. He left a bit ago."

A mix of relief and frustration washed over Elena. Part of her wanted to ask him more about that fateful day, but another part was certain the scene she had envisioned had been the cause of his fiancé's demise. Her grandma, Mai, had told her many a bedtime story that revolved around the spirit world. Being part Chinook Indian with strong ancestral roots to the tribe's shamans made her family a strong conduit for otherworldly energy. Mai had repeatedly sworn to have communicated with the spirit world. Several times, she had told Elena she'd also have the ability, that she could see it in her aura. She had said Elena was open and free and full of love—exactly what spirits in need would seek out.

Could that have been what she'd experienced? It felt entirely too personal. But if so, then why now? And what about her dreams? She'd had them nearly her entire life. Were they related?

Elena had always thought it crazy talk. Stories of lore and fantastical beliefs ingrained from an upbringing on the reservation where part of the family still dressed, spoke, and practiced tradition as often as possible to preserve their culture for future generations. The dreams were strange enough, she could admit, even as she closed her eyes each night and anxiously awaited her return to the world where her mystery woman resided.

But spirits? Watching too many sappy movies had to be the true culprit. Still, it was hard to discount this experience.

Frustration made itself known with a groan, but she pushed a smile to the forefront as Marlie presented her with a beautiful breakfast spread. Her stomach growled. Perhaps a lack of food had played a part, but there was definitely more to it. The first heaping forkful quickly led to another, then another, until she had scarfed the meal down in seconds flat.

Marlie smiled in satisfaction. Her eyes gleamed with "I told you so," though she had never once uttered the words in all the years they'd been friends. Heaven knows she'd certainly had her opportunities. "Judging by the way you devoured that food, I'd say you really do need to eat more often. Feeling better?"

Lifting the napkin to her mouth, Elena wiped as she nodded and replied, "Yes, thanks. You always know best." She set the plate on the counter beside her, which was promptly escorted to the sink by a passing Kit.

"Thanks, Kit."

"No problem." Kit rinsed the dish and set it in the dishwasher, then leaned back and studied Elena. "The color's come back to your face. You looked like you'd seen a ghost."

"I'm feeling much better. It came on so suddenly."

"You're not pregnant, are you?" Kit teased with a wicked laugh. "Just kidding." She swatted her towel at a horrified Elena, then strode past on her way back to work.

"What's she trying to do? Make me pass out again?"

"Oh Elena, being pregnant isn't that bad. I survived one. Now the terrible twos on the other hand..." Marlie nudged her shoulder and laughed.

The joke went unacknowledged as Elena remained stuck on her fear of pregnancy. "Considering I'm a lesbian and that kind of thing doesn't accidentally happen, it's petrifying. Besides, that's never been on my radar. The idea terrifies me."

"Maybe one day, when you meet Miss Right, that'll change."

"Maybe." Elena picked at her nails. "Maybe not. But uh...about that...my dream woman has been more prevalent lately."

"Are you making dreamland babies?"

"Oh my god! No!" Elena's jaw dropped, giving away how very appalling the thought had been. An uncontrollable shiver rocked her body. "It's just as scary there."

Marlie howled with laughter. "You should have seen your face."

"I guess if I manifest that in my dreams next, then I will truly know it's all been my subconscious."

"It is the most plausible answer. Did you talk to Mai yet?"

"No. Though she did give me a dream catcher a few weeks ago." Elena quickly skimmed her memory banks. Interestingly enough, that was roughly the time the dreams had increased.

"Hmmm. You should talk to her."

"I know, but she'll make a big deal over it and they're only dreams."

"If you say so." A long pause fell between them. Marlie shifted awkwardly, then walked back to the stove. "Do you still want to go to Kansas City with me this weekend?" she asked as she cracked a new egg into the griddle.

"Of course. Why wouldn't I?"

"I uh…if you don't feel well, then don't feel obligated."

"I'll be fine. Promise. I'll even come here for breakfast every day so you can be sure I eat right." As if to prove her point, she rose to her feet, thanking the heavens when her legs were strong and steady.

"You just want me to cook for you." Mirth danced in Marlie's eyes as she smirked up at her.

"You're the one who said I needed to eat more, so you set yourself up."

"So, I did. Damn."

"I love that you look out for me." Elena swooped around the stove and wrapped her arms around Marlie from behind. She rested her chin on her best friend's shoulder as she embraced her in an appreciative hug.

"It's what we do for family," Marlie said and tipped her head to touch Elena's.

"I'm so glad we're family."

"Me too."

"Okay, so, I'm going to get back out there. Kit looks overwhelmed." Elena freed Marlie from her embrace and then brushed off her apron.

"I know," Marlie acknowledged, followed by a tired sigh. "One of these days I'll find a reliable server to help her. I can't keep dragging you away from your own work."

"Actually, the change is kind of refreshing. It seems to inspire my creativity and I paint like a woman possessed afterward."

"In that case, work all you want." Marlie grinned wide. "I do appreciate your help."

"I know you do."

"How's the painting going?"

"Great. I sold a few pieces at the gallery and I have several new ones to pitch to a gallery in Seattle. I'm hoping to branch out and get a showing there. We should make it a weekend."

"I'd love to go. I haven't been to Seattle in forever."

"Great. I'll let you know when it's set."

"Okay. I'm glad you're doing that. You never know what adventures await outside the city limits of Portland."

CHAPTER EIGHT

Atlanta - May 10, 2017

Silence hung heavy in Tess's office. She sat across from Rod, assuming their usual positions, but unlike their previous sessions, not a word had been spoken since their greeting. That had been five minutes ago. Since then, she had repressed her urge to ask questions and focused on noting her observations.

Three-day old stubble shaded Rod's face. The spark that had always shone in his light brown eyes was noticeably absent. His mood was morose and his hair and clothing were disheveled. Something had happened since their last session, something big that appeared to have had a monumental and detrimental effect on her client.

Tess glanced at the clock. When six minutes and thirty seconds of silence had been reached, she cleared her throat, hoping it would be a sign to initiate a conversation. The gesture passed without the slightest hint of response. His slumped body and blank stare appeared eerily trance-like.

"Rod?"

No reply. Not even a blink.

Tess tipped her head to catch his line of sight, but he was a million miles away. She leaned forward and snapped her fingers in front of his face, finally bringing him back to reality. "Rod?"

"Hmm?"

"Are you okay?"

He refused a response, so Tess dived right into her usual questions. Maybe it would stimulate some kind of communication. "Have you been able to get her name?"

"Yes, um, it was Mariana," he said, his eyes still blank and unwilling to meet hers.

Tess noted the use of the past tense "was," but decided against acknowledging it at that moment. "Good. Did you get to talk to her?"

"No. It was more like she was talking to herself, you know, like in the third person?"

"I see."

"She sounded distressed. That was three days ago and I haven't heard from her since. That was also when I had my episode."

"Episode? Please explain."

"Pain. So much pain. My entire body. My head was splitting. My chest tightened until I couldn't breathe. I passed out. My mother called nine-one-one. I spent the night in the hospital and missed my appointment with the hypnotist." He ran all ten fingers roughly through his hair in frustration. "Every test was normal. They said it was anxiety, but...I was feeling good. It just struck out of nowhere, no warning. Scariest moment of my life."

"And nothing since?"

"No."

"And no more voice?"

"No. No voice."

"Shouldn't that be a good thing?"

"It should be, right?" He stared at Tess as if waiting for confirmation, then continued when she offered none. "But...it's almost crippling. The emptiness, the feeling of loss...like my heart was ripped out and there's no more reason to live." He leaned forward on his knees and dropped his face into his hands. "I can't shake it. All I do is drink and sleep." His muffled voice dripped with anguish.

Warning signs flashed like crazy.

"I'm thinking of admitting myself to a psychiatric hospital," he said before Tess could suggest a similar option.

"In light of this new condition, I think that would be wise. I'm so very sorry, Rod. I want you to know that I won't give up on you. I want to find an answer."

"But these kinds of things rarely get fixed, right? We just find ways to manage. Maybe I will still have that chance."

"I hope so."

He smiled weakly. "Me too. Thank you for all you've done. You really did help. This was out of everyone's control. Don't feel bad."

But Tess did. She always did. She nodded anyway. After a brief silence, she set her pen and pad down and then stood. Rod followed. "Should I call and have it set up for you?"

"That would be great, thanks. My mom will take me home to get my things."

Another silence. Finally, Tess cleared her throat and opened the door. "Let me know if I can do anything for you."

"Thank you, Doctor Kenner."

"I wish you the best, Rod. Stay strong."

With downcast eyes and his lips pulled tight into a hard line, he gave her a nod and walked away.

∞ ∞ ∞

Tess tossed three pairs of socks into her suitcase, then pulled one back out. White wouldn't go with the suits she was bringing to the conference. She grumbled to herself and flopped back onto her bed. Her mind was stuck on Rod and the sudden shift in his condition. What had she missed? What could she have done better? Tess wasn't giving up hope just yet. She couldn't wait to pick Dr. Greenbaum's brain.

Not ready to resume packing, she picked up her phone and texted Natalie. They had to head to the airport at four to catch their flight to Kansas City. While she didn't particularly love going away to seminars and conferences, she could definitely do with a weekend away from it all. Plus, even though she would spend some after-hours time with Natalie, she'd have her own room and her own space. It had been far too long since that had happened. Being home early today before Amy had been the first time since...she couldn't even remember when. Amy was just always there when she got home.

"Tess? I'm home," Amy called out from downstairs.

Of course. Just like clockwork. So much for alone time. See? The trip was a godsend.

"I'm up here packing," Tess replied and rolled off the bed. She reached for the television remote and turned on the news for some background distraction. Sorting through her shoe collection, she decided on black loafers and her favorites, the black and white wingtips. The rapid, heavy clomp of Amy's heels quickly ascending the stairs carried through the house. Tess's spine stiffened. She picked up the shoes and set them beside her briefcase.

"Hey, Honey," Amy cooed and gave her a quick peck on the lips. "It's so nice to have you home early." Amy kicked her heels off on the way to her side of the closet and set her purse on the dresser.

"It was a rough day and I had to pack for tomorrow."

Amy's mood dampened. "I'm going to miss you."

As frustrated as Tess got with relationships, it was nice to hear those words. "I know, but you can have a girls' weekend with Becky and Rachel. You haven't done that in a long time."

"True. Just don't go too crazy with Nat. I know how she can get." A teasing grin spread across Amy's face.

Tess chuckled. "Don't worry. There won't be a repeat of Dallas. I'll be on my best behavior. Besides, I'll probably have to play wrangler once she gets a couple of drinks in her."

"It will be a hefty chore wrangling her alone."

"Right? Drunk Natalie is like herding cats."

They both laughed. Tess paused to take in the rare light moment between them. She dropped her eyes to the floor and returned to the closet to pick out her suits. When had her mood shifted toward the heavy dread she now carried?

"You're taking those wingtips?" Amy's tone left no mistaking her distaste for the shoes.

Oh yeah, That's when. "You know they're my favorite."

"But it's a professional event."

"And I wear them to my office." Tess let out a frustrated sigh. "Look, I'm not going to argue over them again."

"Fine. If you want to look silly, it's on you," Amy remarked as if Tess were some kind of fool for indulging her own style rather than chasing seasonal fashion trends.

Tess rolled her eyes. The gruff statement would do nothing to change her mind. "Thank you," she replied with heavy sarcasm.

Amy stood by quietly as Tess carefully placed two suits, navy with pinstripes and black, into the garment bag. Tess ignored the uncomfortable silence and focused instead on the news anchor going on and on about all the horrible things that had happened today. That's why she never kept up with the news. It was just a perpetual cycle of all the negativity in the world. No wonder everyone was depressed and angry. Why had she even turned it on? She had her own horrible day to wallow in.

"How about a drink?" Amy finally said.

"Sure," Tess replied, still fiddling with her suits to avoid Amy's stare.

"Okay. The usual?"

Tess couldn't miss the defeated tone. She moved to her dresser, glancing up quickly to flash a smile as she answered, "That would be great. Thanks." She pulled her pajamas from the drawer and returned to her suitcase.

A forced smile preceded Amy's exit. Tess released a hard breath. Were all relationships like this? Whenever this was over, she was never doing it again. In no mood to finish, she groaned and slapped her pajamas down onto the bed. A whiskey and coke sounded great about now.

Desperate for anything to distract her, Tess looked up at the television. A small photo of a Hispanic-looking woman was displayed in the corner. She was attractive with light brown eyes—soft, caring ones—and a bright smile. There was something magnetic about her and Tess felt compelled to listen in. She grabbed the remote and turned up the volume until the female news anchor's voice came in loud and clear.

"The woman killed in a hit and run while biking Monday morning has been identified as twenty-nine-year-old Mariana Lopez."

The name instantly caught Tess's attention. No other words were heard. A ton of lead dropped into her belly and her knees struggled to hold her up. An uncomfortable feeling swarmed in her chest. "Mariana," she whispered. "Spanish female," she continued.

What were the chances? And how? It was too far-fetched.

"Tess, your drink is ready," Amy called up the stairs.

Her mind busy with theories, Tess had barely heard the words.

"Tess?"

"Yeah. Umm...coming," she sputtered. Her body shifted to autopilot. She turned off the television and headed down stairs while her mind bombarded her with questions. How could Rod and Mariana be connected? Could she really have been the voice? It was impossible. But the connection was hard to ignore and the timing of her silence, perfect.

However, no matter how strong the link, Tess's theory would make her a laughing stock. She'd surely lose her license. There had to be another reason. And, even if it were only for her own sanity, she wouldn't quit until she found it.

CHAPTER NINE

Kansas City, Missouri - May 13, 2017

"Come on, Nat, I just want to order room service. I've suffered through a long day of boring speakers and faking smiles." Tess groaned as she tossed her black blazer onto the hotel chair and fell face down onto the bed, crinkling the perfectly crisp comforter. She reached back and freed her long hair from the captivity of her bun.

"Did you forget I was there too? That's exactly why it'll be good for you. You're getting boring. I miss 'grad school Tess.' She was fun." Natalie turned to the mirror, admiring the sew-in weave she'd gotten yesterday. She slipped her fingers under her new long, curly blonde locks and gave it a fluff until she was happy with the way it laid. Her skin tone contrasted nicely between the light hair and dark skirt suit.

"Liar. I wasn't any different back then." Tess's rebuttal was muffled by the comforter.

"But you were." Natalie turned back to Tess's prone form on the bed. "All right, so you didn't run wild, but you were always up for a drink and down for a hookup."

Tess turned her head and stared at Natalie before a heavy breath was blown through her puffed cheeks. "I'm with Amy." The words carried the weight of an anchor, echoing her feelings about the relationship. Even as she'd said it, she realized how badly it had sounded. Adding up the weeks in her head, it had only been six or so. "You know what I mean."

"Yes. Unfortunately, I do," was uttered, accompanied by an exhausted sigh. "You tell me everything. But I was only talking about drinks, Tess."

"Fine." It came out in a huff. "But you had better be buying me some great barbeque to go with those drinks."

"You're so easy. Next time, I'll lead with food." When Tess made no move to get up, Natalie walked to the bed and gave her a nudge in the form of a healthy swat on the butt. "Let's go."

"Ouch! I'm going." Tess's roll off the bed was less than enthusiastic. "Nothing too late though. It's already hard enough to sit through the conference and the one speaker I wanted to see didn't show." Her mood had plummeted since the announcement of Dr. Greenbaum's absence. It seemed she couldn't catch a break and neither could Rod. She'd have to try and contact the doctor through his foundation.

Grabbing a hair tie off the nightstand, her hands went immediately to the deep brown locks that reached her mid-back and sharply pulled them back into a tight ponytail.

"Maybe they should hire professional speakers to read the research papers, like a comedian." Natalie laughed. "What do you think?"

Tess smiled and shrugged. She slipped one arm into her blazer and then the other. As she went to leave, a quick decision to change shoes sent her to the closet. She loved her wingtips, but this was casual time. "Couldn't be much worse. I'll keep it in mind next time I'm asked to present. Lord knows, I'm a boring speaker." After slipping into her black leather loafers, she grabbed her wallet and room key, and headed to the door.

"I'll be sure to remind you."

"I know you will. Now, where are you dragging me off to?"

"The Power and Light District. It's just across the way. They have an indoor-outdoor bar and restaurant area. It's a good time. I checked it out last visit. But first, I promised barbeque, so we'll head to Plowboys."

The elevator ride was stuffed full of suits that had attended the conference. Tess remained silent, only scrunching her face as she threw an unamused glare at Nat. Her fingers clenched and unclenched repeatedly in time with a steady counting of Mississippi's in her head. The moment the door opened, Tess wriggled her way free and walked briskly through the ornate lobby of the Hilton, leaving Natalie jogging to catch up.

"Whoa, Tess. I've still got my heels on."

"That's a problem I never have," Tess stated plainly as her pace quickened across the white tiled floor. She burst through the doors into the cool night air and came to a stop, inhaling a deep breath. As she exhaled, she gave Natalie an apologetic look. "Sorry. You know I'm claustrophobic."

"Yep. Even in relationships."

"Funny," Tess snarked. "Tell me you enjoy being stuck in a metal box that can send you plummeting to your death."

"I don't enjoy elevators, but I don't have a response to getting into one either. Between your fear of elevators and commitment, you'd make a fascinating study in our field. I should write a paper about you."

The glare returned, hardened by narrowed eyes that only made Natalie laugh out loud. "Relax. Let's get you some food and several drinks. You've lost your sense of humor. Jeeze." She looped her arm into the crook of Tess's elbow and led them down the street. "You know, they say many of the professionals in our field are worse than their clients."

"I've heard that too."

"Maybe it's transference. I mean, we can't possibly be around that much dysfunction and not have some of it rub off, right?"

"I don't know. I'm not sure I believe in that."

"My massage therapist swears that when a bunch of people come in with similar problems for her to work on, she ends up going home with the same problem."

Tess considered the statement for a moment. There were plenty of studies proving that if you really believed in something, you could convince yourself of its truth. There were various opinions on how it worked, but in the end, a person believed what they wanted to believe, even to the point of physical symptoms, as evidenced by the placebo effect. "Interesting. Definitely sounds like a psychological component."

"Possibly. But don't you believe in physical energy transference?"

She tipped her head, catching sight of Natalie with a sideways glance. "Never really thought about it." She shrugged. "But I don't think it happens like that."

"What about reincarnation? Fate? Soul mates?" A perfectly penciled brow arched, punctuating her question.

A throaty laugh rumbled up from Tess's chest. She was not getting into that debate. "That's a whole other realm, Natalie. That's spiritual belief."

"It's still energy. The soul is energy. That's what I believe."

"I'm not very spiritual, sorry."

"Right. Just science for you. I forgot."

Tess shrugged and turned her attention back to the sidewalk ahead. As they passed a window on the right, a flash of color caught her eye. She paused and stared at the back of a dark-haired woman inside, only catching what appeared to be some kind of bird tattoo on her left shoulder blade before it was covered by a tan jacket. Quick to catch herself, she turned and caught up to Natalie, but glanced back over her shoulder. Her pulse quickened and her skin danced with electricity, both reactions unexpected and foreign to her. That empty place in her heart dared her to try and fill it—something she had never thought possible.

"What? What's wrong?" Natalie's head swiveled around, never breaking stride.

"Nothing. It's fine," Tess sputtered as she pressed on. Nothing except for the odd compulsion to turn back. There was a swelling of unexplainable desire to meet this complete stranger, another thing she had never experienced before. She tried to push it aside, to continue on their path to Plowboys, but it niggled in her mind and in her belly.

Five steps past the establishment's entrance, Tess could ignore it no longer. "Let's check this out." She tugged Natalie around by the hand and led her back to the entrance, only to be met by a long line of customers waiting to be carded and let inside.

Nearly tumbling over as her heel caught in a sidewalk crack, a frazzled Natalie asked, "This is where I was going to take you, but I thought you wanted to eat first? I remember you specifically asking for barbeque." One hand steadied her against Tess's shoulder, while she checked the integrity of her heel with the other.

Tess let out a grunt as she braced to support the added weight. She strained her neck to see past the crowd. "It's Kansas City. There's probably barbeque everywhere. But this line…"

Natalie righted herself, then remarked, "You're being weird." Her hands smoothed over the sides of her black skirt and blazer, making sure everything was in order.

The statement gave Tess pause. She spun around and met the intense hazel-eyed gaze of her old friend. Was that a look of apprehension? Or was it concern? Was there reason to be worried? *Pfft. Not at all. Just curious.* "No, I'm not. But I decided I didn't want to walk all over the place. It's bad enough you've dragged me out."

Suspicion coated Natalie's expression, but she relented, her aggressive posture relaxing as she grumbled, "Okay…fine. Just be patient. I'm sure it won't be long."

Patience? Patience had been made hostage behind a triple locked door. Tess had never needed to get anywhere as fast as she did right now and she couldn't even explain why. As discreetly as possible, her eyes rolled over the crowd and skimmed through each and every face in search of the woman.

I am being weird. What the hell am I doing?

No answer presented itself, just an all-consuming need to meet the woman face to face. She tore her eyes away and returned them to Natalie, who was still watching her with unabashed curiosity. Tess quickly looked away and fished her phone from her pocket, using it as an excuse to busy herself.

"Mhm." Natalie mumbled unamused. She crossed her arms and kicked out her left hip, her foot tapping and tapping and tapping until Tess finally acknowledged her.

"What?" Tess asked, never abandoning her view of the phone's bright screen. Her fingers swiped away at anything and everything that could divert her eyes from Natalie.

"You're looking for a woman, aren't you? Someone caught your fancy."

"That's ridiculous. I have-"

"Amy. Yes, I know. I also know you're not happy with Amy. You don't really like doing the relationship thing."

"Your knack for listening to me can be annoying."

"Believe me, it can be a chore."

A relationship conversation was the last thing Tess wanted to delve into...well, that and the spirituality thing, but there was one thing she wanted to make crystal clear. She turned off her screen, shoved her phone into her jacket pocket, and then stood tall. "Look, I may not be happy, but I'm also not a cheater."

"I never said you were," Natalie clarified.

"But that's what your statement infers," Tess replied matter-of-factly.

Natalie rolled her eyes but didn't back down. "Your knack for dissecting my statements can be annoying."

"Believe me, it can be a chore."

Natalie stared in silence for long seconds until the people behind them nudged them forward. They were almost to the front.

"So...?"

"Fine," Tess huffed and shook her head. "Yes. I saw a woman quickly through the glass. She had this bright bird tattoo. For some reason, I just had the urge to see her up close. I don't know if I would talk to her or not, but..." she sighed and rubbed her face, "you're right. I'm being weird. Let's go to Plowboys."

Tess stepped out of line, but Natalie grabbed her arm and pulled her back in. "Oh, no you don't. We're next. May as well go and see if we can find her. Now I'm curious to see what kind of woman grabs your attention so raptly."

Tess's face twisted into a grimace, but her heart skipped at the thought. Excitement bubbled in her chest. She was curious too. That's why they had gotten into line. She already knew the woman wasn't anything like her usual type. The stranger was tattooed, for one thing. Then, there was the bold hairstyling with the sides cut into a fade—a one-eighty from the long, perfectly groomed tresses that usually graced Tess's pillows. She was also medium height rather than tall. And finally, she was curvy as opposed to thin, but Tess had found the swell of the woman's hips and backside quite sexy. She had been so consumed with her thoughts she hadn't registered actually entering the venue.

"Okay. Where to?" Natalie stood hands on hips, surveying their surroundings. Several restaurants and bars lined the edge, all bustling with energy and bodies. The center bar was also packed, as well as the area around the fire pits. There was not an empty seat to be found.

Clarity returned and Tess led Natalie in the direction she had last seen the tattooed stranger. Anxiousness roused every nerve ending and twirled in her belly as they began a thorough sweep of the venue. A half an hour later, Natalie had disappeared, their search had come up empty, and the bubbles of wondrous possibility had gone flat.

Tess was at a loss over the feeling of emptiness inside. She had never been one to get so caught up over a woman, much less any "love at first sight" phenomenon. Heck, for that matter, it was only half a sight—the back half. Even so, it felt as if she had missed out on something monumental. She sighed and shook her head. It made no sense.

Natalie re-appeared with a Jack and Coke in each hand. "Sorry you didn't find her." She extended one to Tess, who accepted and quickly took several big gulps to drown her sorrows.

"Yeah well..." Tess stared at her drink. Her soul seemed half-empty, just like her cup. With her mind muddled in a state of confusion, she tried to ponder her expectations. She came up with nothing really, though a part of her deep down inside had evidently planned for something grand. "It's for the best. I mean, what was going to happen anyway?"

"Light conversation. An enjoyable evening. Make a new friend. Who knows?"

"Eh." She played it off, but couldn't believe it would have been that bland. Not the way she was feeling. But now, she would never know.

Natalie laughed, which then morphed into a feral growl that drew Tess's attention. "What?"

"Look at that delicious man." She practically drooled as a tall, dusty blond with an athletic build strutted by.

"Not interested. Besides, you're married."

"Married, not dead."

"Some may argue the opposite."

"Very funny. You know I'd never act on it, but damned if I can't look. Like when I did the keto diet and we walked past that French bakery."

"As I recall, that was the day the diet ended." Tess spotted two seats at the bar being vacated and hurried over.

Natalie trotted up and not-so-gracefully slid into one, slightly spilling her drink and nearly missing the chair all together.

Tess suppressed a laugh but not her wide grin. Had Natalie been doing shots at the bar while waiting for their drinks?

Smoothly remaining on topic and ignoring her faux pas, Natalie admitted, "Okay, bad example, but I didn't jump on the first yummy apple tart I saw."

"No. I believe it took five," Tess confirmed with a sarcastic half-smirk.

"Hmm…good. So, I can look at three more guys before I need to worry about it."

"Sound logic," Tess deadpanned. Her smirk worked its way toward the corners of her mouth, but was derailed by finishing off her drink.

"See. That's the Tess I remember."

"I admit that it's nice to be out. Thank you for ignoring my whining."

"You're welcome. How about a refill?"

"Sure, as long as there's food included."

With a laugh and a nod, Natalie touched her glass and held up two fingers to the bartender who had looked their way. She handed Tess a menu that had been left behind. "Whatever you want, as long it's on the happy hour menu."

"Wow. You're too good to me," Tess said with a humorous glint in her eyes.

"I try. Now, whatever kind of trouble shall we get into tonight?"

Tess shrugged. She no longer cared, as long as it took her mind off the woman with the bird tattoo.

CHAPTER TEN

Marlie locked her arm in Elena's to steady them both as they weaved their way through the crowd toward the exit. Elena couldn't keep herself from laughing, a not-so-subtle sign that she had had too much to drink. It had been a while since they'd had a girl's night out and she made a mental note to not wait so long again.

"That was so much fun, Marlie. Thanks for letting me tag along this weekend."

"You're always welcome. Hey, when's the last time we went out anyway?"

"I don't know." Elena's mouth quirked up and to the left as she searched for an answer. "I think over the holidays. This was the first year we didn't even go out for New Year's. We should definitely do it again soon though."

"Agreed. Ugh! I wish I didn't have to go back to the conference tomorrow."

"Me too, but hey, tomorrow you get an award for small business of the year and that's awesome." Elena beamed with pride.

"Thanks. I appreciate it, but you know, I'm just trying to do my part to make women-owned businesses more visible and successful. That's why I joined the Women's Business Association to start with."

"Well, you are succeeding and I applaud you."

"Aww. You're going to make me teary. You know how I get when I drink."

Elena laughed and gave Marlie's arm a gentle tug to hang a right as they exited the building. They walked past a large window that looked into the restaurant they had just left. The urge to look inside rushed through her. Her skin tingled, just as it had a bit ago when they were inside. She turned and peered through the glass, catching a quick glance of the side of a dark-haired woman wearing a dark suit before she disappeared into the crowd.

Elena had always been a sucker for a woman in a suit, but she was drawn to this one more than most. The thought of going back inside flitted through her mind. She could buy her a drink, see if her eyes were blue. Who knew what would come after.

It wasn't only her curiosity that had been piqued, her body reacted as well. Goosebumps prickled her skin. The beat of her heart stumbled before breaking into a sprint. Shallow breaths were all she could muster as she came to the end of the window, losing any chance of seeing the mystery woman again.

Unless she decided to go back inside.

Marlie stumbled, but Elena was quick to return to her senses, keeping her friend upright with a firm grip. There was only one place they should be going and that was back to the hotel. Though her body protested, all thought of talking up the stranger faded into the background, joining the pile of other wishful thoughts that had gathered over the years.

Fifteen minutes later, both of them buzzed and tired, they dragged themselves into their hotel room. Marlie kicked her shoes off, dropped her pants on the floor, and unhooked her bra from under her shirt. She fell unceremoniously backward onto the bed, passing out cold the second her body landed.

Elena tucked her under the covers, smiling at the woman who was like a sister to her. *What would I do without her?* She made her way quietly to the bathroom, stopping to undress along the way—shirt tossed to the floor, her pants in a ball with her sneakers, and her bra beside them. After a swish of mouthwash, she slipped into her sleep shirt and shorts and then climbed into bed expecting the alcohol to send her into dreamland as quickly as it had Marlie. Instead, she lay staring at the ceiling.

The odd feeling from earlier still had every cell in her brain and body in a tizzy. A need to find real life proof of the woman in her dreams had reared its head and driven her curiosity about the woman at the bar. There had been such a need to act thrumming through her, but the timing had been all wrong. What would have been the point anyway? They probably lived on opposite ends of the country or she would have been married.

Still, her body remained revved at high RPM's, heated to the core as if the stranger's hands were on her, caressing her skin, and inside her, driving her to unimaginable heights. She released a ragged breath with a shudder as she allowed her eyes to close.

Thinking was stressing out her mind and her imagination had her physically exhausted, yet she was wired to the max. Oh, how she wished she had more alcohol in her room to calm the storm. Sleep was her happy place and like every other day, she had been longing for another date with her blue-eyed beauty. Elena just hoped it would come soon.

∞ ∞ ∞

Light shone through the hotel curtains, nudging Elena from sleep. Her eyes cracked open and the haze of too many fruity drinks clouded her vision. That uncomfortable morning longing she had become so accustomed to settled in. Yet another day had arrived without the one person she wanted most by her side. A low groan crawled from her throat as she rolled away from the sun. Marlie was asleep in the next bed, lying flat on her back, mouth wide open, and left arm over her head.

She stifled a laugh and closed her eyes, drifting back into the realm between dreams and reality—the place she was most at peace. Fragments of last night's dream returned. A grin claimed possession of her lips and a soft whimper of want trickled out.

Brilliant blue eyes the color of sapphires smiled at her. A tiny mole sat above the woman's left brow. Dark brown hair cascaded over broad shoulders. Strong arms locked possessively around Elena's waist. They stared into one another's eyes, silent and comfortable, an aura of love their cocoon. Elena's hands gripped the edges of a gray vest, pulling them closer until their mouths were a whisper apart.

First, barely a brush. Then, a gentle interlocking of soft warm lips. Finally, fireworks. They sparked behind her eyelids and crackled in her belly, setting her body on fire and sending her heart rate rocketing.

A gentle, but determined hand caressed her cheek, then stroked a path between her breasts and down her belly, stealing her breath as it dipped lower, slipping underneath her jeans on its way to a destination they were both anxious to reach.

BEEP! BEEP! BEEP!

SLAM!

"Shut up," Marlie grumbled. She fumbled with the alarm until it shut off and then rolled away.

Elena's eyes flew open wide. Rapid, shallow breaths accompanied a sweat peppered neck and a pulse pounding in her throat. Her libido remained locked in high gear, causing her thighs to clench and a whimper to escape at being left high and not so dry. Realization struck and she sank into the bed. The touch she had craved all night had been ripped away before its fulfillment.

Sadness swallowed her whole, turning the light to darkness much the way the sun did the moon each month. Her eyes sealed shut. A tear trickled out. The moment was gone. Again. Another day had arrived, bringing with it her waking up alone and wanting…so very wanting. Her skin still burned where the hand had traveled. Her lips tingled. If she concentrated hard enough, she could taste those delicious full lips. So real, yet not at all.

Elena rolled out of bed and padded to the bathroom. A cold shower was in order. As much as she'd love to return to her dream, waking always left her with a longing ache, sometimes for hours afterward. Losing her beloved dream girl a third time in one morning would just be cruel and unusual punishment.

CHAPTER ELEVEN

Lake Helen, Georgia - June 3, 2017

"Tess, honey, are you ready?" Amy called out from the front porch of the cabin.

"Just a second." Tess buckled her belt, grabbed her backpack, and walked toward the porch, taking in the sight of her girlfriend's gigantic smile as she approached. Amy's happiness was contagious and it helped Tess dismiss the uneasiness that had been making her twitchy since they'd headed north last night. "Okay, I'm all set. Where to today?"

"I thought we'd drive up to Bryson City and hit the Smokies for a day trip."

The uneasiness returned with a vengeance, sending a shiver racing up her spine. When it reached the top, it ripped a U-turn and sped right back down. Tess choked back the peculiar dread with a forced smile. "Sounds nice."

Amy sucked in a deep breath of cool mountain air, oblivious to her plight. *Good.* The trip was supposed to be a fun weekend for them to bond, or whatever, so Tess hoped to keep her newfound discomfort hidden the rest of the trip. She'd start by shoving her fidgeting fingers into her back pockets. For the life of her, she could neither explain, nor pinpoint, the cause. Anxiety had never been one of her character traits. Was it intuition? Would something bad happen? She certainly hoped that wouldn't be the case. Maybe it was doing the "girlfriend" thing with Amy that had thrown her off. This had been her longest relationship since high school, so Tess hadn't done a weekend getaway in years. Yep. That had to be it.

Taking a cue from Amy, Tess partook in a large intake of fresh air. The early morning mist over the trees was a work of art and the quiet...only the sound of the light breeze rustling the leaves reached her ears. The east coast mountains were so different than the ones in Colorado where she and Evan had visited as children. Back then, she had loved the mountains and would go every chance she got, but in the twenty years since she'd lived in Atlanta, she seemed to have an aversion to them. Until now, she hadn't noticed how much she had missed them. If only this gnawing inside would go away, she could really enjoy herself.

Tess adjusted her pack on her shoulder, then walked to Amy's bright orange Nissan Murano. She pecked Amy on the lips before tossing her pack in the backseat and settling into the passenger side. Her right knee began a rapid bob up and down. Not wanting Amy to notice, she quickly silenced it with her hand, forcing the limb into submission until the nervous energy migrated from her leg upward into her chest, speeding her heart rate to a dizzying pace.

"Here we go," Amy said as she settled in behind the wheel. She smiled at Tess and then started the engine.

Tess forced her best smile in return, hoping she didn't look like a crazed lunatic, because boy, did she sure ever feel like one. As they started their drive, she took deep, quiet breaths and talked herself down. Everything would be fine. If she said it enough times, studies proved she'd eventually believe it. It was just a casual day out. Fun. She could do fun. It had been a while, but it wasn't rocket science. She'd smile and relax and if nothing else, dammit, she'd fake it till she made it.

∞ ∞ ∞

There was little conversation during the ride. Any time Amy got into a car she transformed into a professional singer complete with all the moves, though she lacked an audibly pleasing tone. It could be entertaining at times, but Tess would prefer she kept her hands on the wheel while navigating the windy two-lane highway. The mile after mile of tree-lined roads became hypnotic as Tess stared out the window. She lost track of all time, only taking note of the Smoky Mountain National Park sign as they turned onto U.S. Route 441.

"We made good time, so we can stop and have lunch at one of the overlooks before hitting the Blue Ridge Parkway."

Tess's stomach growled causing them both to laugh.

"I'll take that as a sign of agreement."

"I'd say so." Tess patted her belly. "Thanks for driving."

"No problem. I hope you can actually relax and enjoy it. You've been working too hard." The sadness behind Amy's smile was impossible to miss, though she did a good job of keeping it from hindering her words.

"Sorry." Tess would never admit that a big part of those long work hours had been relationship avoidance. The excitement of their new relationship had worn off quickly. Now, it seemed all she ever did was hurt Amy. As much as she had tried to push her away, however, Amy had fought for her. Tess had no idea why. She didn't deserve that kind of dedication, but this weekend she was really going to try to make things right.

"I am enjoying this, Amy. Really. It's beautiful. This was a great idea." Her statement had Amy smiling wide and genuine. Tess hadn't seen such light in Amy's eyes in weeks and it had been all her fault. The realization made her feel like more of an ass than usual and stirred her to double her efforts. This would be a make or break weekend for them. Though she had always been rooting for the break, Amy's efforts and affability had awakened Tess's typically absent conscience with a smack right between the eyes. What other woman would try so hard to make her happy?

A few miles up the road, Amy veered off at a sign for Mingo Falls. It was a busy day at the scenic stop, forcing them to creep along behind each group who appeared to be leaving in hunt of a parking space. Finally securing a spot, they grabbed their picnic basket and set off in search of the perfect place to relax.

Unfortunately, that relaxation didn't come until after a grueling, according to Tess, third of a mile trek up a gazillion steps to reach the falls. When Amy reached the top, she smiled triumphantly with the picnic basket held firm in her right hand. Tess, however, bent over hands on knees, huffing and puffing to refill her poor starving lungs. Once an avid workout fan, it was glaringly apparent that her eight-month excuse-filled hiatus needed to end.

When she had recovered enough to stand, Tess walked over to her snickering girlfriend and leaned against the railing beside her. "This had better be good," she grumbled breathlessly.

"It will be. I promise." Amy kissed her cheek and gave her another moment to recover before asking, "You ready?"

Tess nodded and then stood up on wobbly legs. She followed Amy toward the far side and out onto a giant boulder along the stream. It was indeed beautiful. As she did a three-sixty to take in all the sights, she growled when her eyes reached the steps. The return trip would not be fun.

When a tug on her pant leg brought her attention downward, her future agony was all but forgotten. Amy had set out lunch and made herself comfortable with her bare feet dangling in the water. Tess smiled, remembering her goal of the day. *Make Amy happy and have a little fun.* Being surrounded by the sounds of nature, basking in the colors of the foliage, and embracing the serenity that accompanied the mountains did indeed fill her with a sense of energy that had been missing from her life.

Feeling more like herself than she had in a long time, she sat down, removed her shoes, and dipped her toes into the frigid water. She yanked them out as a shiver raced through her. Ignoring her laughing girlfriend, she dropped them in again, this time to the ankle. The cold was soothing and something more. A sort of wholeness filled her being. She didn't question the sensation, only welcomed it and vowed to return again soon.

∞ ∞ ∞

Lunch had been a wonderful reprieve from her own mind and Tess found she didn't need to fake enjoying her time with Amy. Getting away from the rush of the city had given her new clarity. Maybe relationships weren't all bad. It was nice doing things with someone else. There was only one problem. Somewhere during their enjoyable lunch, Tess had come to accept a cold, hard truth. She didn't love Amy. Well, that wasn't the big revelation, she'd known that all along. The thing that caught her by surprise was that she *couldn't* love her. Try as she may, Tess had no answer, scientific, philosophical, or spiritual, to explain why. Given her situation, she had long since accepted that she somehow lacked the tools to do that one little thing in life. She had never thought of herself as cold-hearted, despite some of her exes' words to the contrary, but if she couldn't love someone as endearing as Amy, then what was her problem? Maybe they'd been right.

Her thoughts drifted to Rod and his words when discussing the need to find a mate in life, before he had lost all interest in living life at all. "Who doesn't?" he had asked so casually, as if it wasn't a predominant concern for many people. But Tess had never had that drive. There seemed to be an empty space that took up most of her chest, allowing only room for her natural born family and work, but nothing more. Over the years, she had come to accept that emptiness as her norm and she was fine with that, but now, she was having her doubts.

So wrapped in her thoughts, Tess hardly noticed packing up and walking back down the steps, but when they neared the car and she snapped back to reality, her tired legs made themselves known with a screaming ache. *Stupid steps.* She couldn't wait to sit down. As they reached the car, Amy touched her back, then slid her hand around and opened the door. The look of adoration in her eyes now made Tess uncomfortable in a new way, but she hoped she was doing a good job of pretending the feeling was returned. She accepted the lack of negative response to mean she had been successful. Amy was most likely too blinded by the air of the romantic lunch by the falls to notice anyway.

Tess settled into her seat and sent a silent thanks to any and all gods listening for giving her legs a reprieve. The rest of the day should consist of mostly driving, which was great. The views were gorgeous. Amy's singing on the other hand, not so much. With that in mind, she greedily added an addendum to her thank you, pleading for them to have mercy on her ears as well.

CHAPTER TWELVE

Thus far, the gods had not favored her second request. Tess cringed when Amy hit a particularly high note, one her voice should definitely never attempt again. But when Amy smiled her way, she forced one in return, gave her a thumbs-up, and pretended to bob her head along with the beat. Tess did her best to drown out the screeching by humming some classic sixties songs and tuning her focus to catch quick peeks at the vast mountain range between every break in the tree-lined road. She had been mildly successful. That was as good as a win.

They had been cruising the park highway at slow speeds to take in as much of the landscape as possible. Smaller roads intersected with their own along the way. One such road, marked by a sign for Rocky Hill Church, oddly and unexpectedly grabbed Tess's attention. Her stomach turned. Bile bubbled into her esophagus. She shifted uncomfortably in her seat and took a quick swig of water. That helped, but only momentarily. Like lava rising into the throat of a volcano before eruption, her lunch ebbed and flowed as it churned, climbing higher the further they traveled up the hill. At the apex, a sharp curve. Tess couldn't take it any longer. There wasn't much room between the road and the guardrail, but she needed out. Fast.

"Stop!"

"What?" Amy swerved, startled by the sudden outburst. She barely missed slamming into the rail. Her wide eyes and high brows of shock plummeted to fear and concern at the sight of Tess doubled over in her seat.

"Stop, now!" Tess shouted again, quickly bringing a hand to cover her mouth.

Before the car could come to a complete halt, Tess unsnapped her seatbelt and flung open the door. Vomit spewed across the highway's white line and onto the grass. She sprung from the car toward the railing that overlooked the ledge. One look at the bottom sent her to her knees.

Paralyzing loss. Heart break. Guilt. A tsunami of emotions without reason engulfed her.

The feelings rolled through her again and again, crashing hard and fast like waves against an ocean cliff. Dizziness forced her to steady herself on the cool metal rail. She looked to the right. Two small crosses sat at the ledge. The words were long gone and the paint had faded. Only worn wood remained a symbol where someone who was loved had been lost.

Again, Tess was crippled by the emotions for which she had no basis. Her vision blurred, then became crystal clear, but she was no longer on her knees at the guardrail.

She was airborne, plunging toward the bottom of the cliff. The metal hood of an old, red truck stood out among the view of green trees and gray storm clouds whipping past. Her stomach lifted into her throat with such force no sound could be uttered, yet a scream throttled her eardrums, piercingly loud. Covering her ears did nothing to drown it out, just as covering her eyes did nothing to dull the violent impact that sent her body crumbling to the ground.

Rolling. Crashing. Metal crinkling under the force of earth's obstacles.

Then, silence. The odor of gasoline, exhaust, and dirt stung her nose. A sputtering groan forced her eyes open once again. Dust and smoke combined to create a heavy fog around her, but in the center seat, the driver's trembling hand covered the passenger's bloodied, limp one—women's hands. A pained and broken "I'm sorry" was uttered. Blackness prevailed.

Heavy sobs wracked Tess's body. Though she had no earthly idea who the women were, it all felt so very personal, as if she herself had been the reason for their death. She wretched as Amy reached her side in a panic.

"Tess? Tess, are you okay?"

"I- I...It's-" She wretched again. Her entire body convulsed. There were no words to describe the worst feeling she had ever experienced. Worse than losing her parents or her best friend, an eleven-year-old black lab mix, Moose.

Amy helped her into a seated position and held her tight, crying along with her. "It's okay," she soothed and gently stroked small circles on Tess's back. "It's okay. I got you."

The flowery scent of Amy's Coco Mademoiselle perfume brought Tess back to the present and the hard, rocky roadside she was seated on. Her scientific mind scoured for explanations, but came up empty again and again.

"I'm sorry," she said, her heart seizing as the familiar words left her mouth. Those were two words that would forever haunt her through no fault of her own. A wave of nausea made a return and she took a deep breath in hopes of calming herself.

"Here." Amy handed her a bottle of water.

Tess raised the bottle to her mouth and sipped slowly as she observed their surroundings. Just a two-lane road, a Route 441 sign, and Mother Nature. There was nothing to note, unless you counted the horrified expression on her girlfriend's face. She attempted to get to her feet, but her legs were as wobbly as the time she had decided to run stadium steps.

"Let me help you." Amy stood and took Tess's hand, aiding her effort with a heave of her own. She circled around, knocking the dust from Tess's clothes before fixing her own. "Are you all right? Should we find a hospital or something?"

Tess ignored her and stepped back to the ledge. There was some deep-seated need to see the bottom again, though she couldn't explain why and dreaded a return episode of what she had just suffered through. Whatever had overcome her had been the most terrifying experience of her life, but not enough to keep her from the ledge.

When she reached the rail, she looked down, then breathed a sigh of relief that her legs remained steady and her stomach calm.

"Tess?"

She looked back at Amy, who stood petrified, carefully watching her every move. "No. I think I'm fine, but let's turn around." She didn't want to find out if there were any other surprises up ahead.

"Sure. Okay." Amy released a sigh of relief. "We can head back to the cabin."

One look at Amy and Tess could tell she still wanted to tour. In truth, she did too. She had been having a good time earlier. "Or we could go a different way?" she offered. "Head back and try another route? But I'd like to stop at the store and grab something for my stomach."

"If you think you're feeling well enough, then we can do that, but if you get sick again, I'm taking you to the hospital right away," Amy asserted.

"And I won't argue."

"At first, I thought it was food poisoning, but then I was afraid you were having a seizure. You scared me to death, Tess." The slight tremble of Amy's hands backed up her confession.

"I'm-" No. Tess wouldn't say those words ever again. Instead, she opted for, "Me too."

"I hope it wasn't the deviled eggs I made. I was sure I kept them cool enough."

"I'm pretty sure they had nothing to do with it." Amy smiled and Tess offered her hand, which was eagerly accepted. Tess pulled her in close and pressed a kiss to her forehead. "I probably just ate too much and then did all those steps. Thank you for taking care of me."

"Always." Amy wrapped her arms around Tess's waist in comfort.

They remained in the warm embrace for several long seconds until Tess was ready to tear herself away. As she buckled herself back into the passenger seat, she chanced one last glance at the pair of wooden crosses. Again, her chest ached and incomprehensible loss filled her soul. Empty. That was the best word she could find to describe her feeling as Amy turned the car around and drove away. Empty like that space in her heart that couldn't seem to be filled by anyone or anything. But why? Why did that space exist? And why in hell did that place make her feel it so very deeply?

∞ ∞ ∞

Tess shot up straight in bed, her chest heaving and sweat soaking through her shirt and shorts. Darkness engulfed her, save for a sliver of full moon peeking through the gap in the curtains.

She wiped her brow and took a deep breath as she re-oriented herself to their rented cabin.

Amy lay sleeping peacefully beside her. *Lucky girl.* A good night's sleep might never be had by Tess again. The sound of crunching metal still echoed in her head. The vile sight of the bloodied hand still made her sick to her stomach. But it was the anguish in the strangled "I'm sorry" that refused to release its grip on her chest, squeezing until breath seemed it may never visit her again.

She slid carefully from the bed and tiptoed to the small kitchen. There had to be something to soothe her nerves. They'd finished the wine last night and since she hadn't been feeling well earlier, they had passed on picking up more. A whiskey would be perfect, but no such luck. Chocolate would have to suffice.

She slipped a piece of Dove dark from the bag and then paused. Not that chocolate wasn't a cure all, but Tess had really hoped for something a bit more...potent. Okay, three chocolates would have to do. She grabbed two more of the foil wrapped goodies and padded to the bathroom so as not to disturb her girlfriend.

Quietly as she could, she unwrapped the first chocolate, popped it into her mouth, then sighed in relief—instant gratification in its purest form. She sat on the edge of the tub and unwrapped the second one, pushing away thoughts of how the metallic sound of the foil wrapper reminded her of the twisting metal haunting her dreams.

But her dream had been different than the hallucination at the cliff. This time, there had been more to the story. Rain was pouring down. They were being pursued. The driver lost control and...

She didn't need to revisit the rest again. Question was, why did she ever visit in the first place? There was no scientific reason for her sudden condition and she wasn't having a stroke. Not that she believed in hauntings, but there was some solid scientific evidence to support such stories. Could it be the anniversary of their death or some other notable moment that stirred spirits who'd left this plane too soon?

"Ridiculous," Tess muttered, then unwrapped the last piece of dark chocolate joy. Another sigh escaped when she placed it into her mouth and she rolled her eyes at its silky deliciousness. As she swallowed the last of it down, the reality of her fatigue set in. The day had been a trying one and sleep would be a wonderful gift. Though she didn't believe in spirits, she'd try anything to get some restful shuteye.

"Look," she started, hardly believing what she was about to do. "I feel for you both, I really do. Whatever it was that happened to you..." she paused to find the words she wanted, then finished, "it was tragic." Her eyes squeezed shut, stamping out tears that threatened to fall as a swell of emotion arose. "I could feel the love and the loss and it was heartbreaking," she admitted through a shuddering breath. "I truly hope you find peace, but I can't help you. I can't. So please, please…I need sleep."

A light breeze filtered under the door, just enough to draw Tess's attention, then faded, seemingly taking with it her distress. She felt inexplicably lighter. Tess gnawed her lower lip as she analyzed what had happened. Surely, it was all some sort of subconscious manifestation. Talking out loud could do wonders to ease stress.

Yes. That was most certainly it and not some paranormal experience. Those kinds of thoughts would make her a laughing stock. Regardless of how unbelievably real and totally cryptic the day had been, she would be keeping it all to herself.

Tess stood up, tossed the wrappers away, and quietly put herself back to bed. This time, sleep came easy and it was every bit as peaceful as she had requested.

CHAPTER THIRTEEN

Seattle, Washington – June 25, 2017

A car horn honked and their cab driver huffed to make sure his annoyance was known. Tess ignored them both and said, "I have to run back in." Her words fast and her emotions flustered, she continued to frantically tear apart her carry-on bag in the trunk of the cab. She was looking for…. she wasn't sure what exactly, but something was missing. Something she needed.

"Come on, Tess. We're already running late. We'll miss our flight." Warren lifted one end of Tess's open suitcase and settled his underneath.

"Relax. We'll make it. Just hang on. I'll only be a sec." Clueless as to the missing item she couldn't live without, Tess couldn't let the nagging feeling go. She was ninety-nine percent sure she had everything packed, thanks to her methodical sweep of the room, but something kept pulling her back inside.

She ran to the counter of the Waterfront Marriott Hotel and was quickly given back her key. Her black and white wingtips clacked against the tiled floor as she trotted to the elevators.

Fortunately, one was ready and waiting. She pressed the fifth-floor button and smoothed out her black tailored suit. A light sweat formed under her white button-down. She groaned. Soggy undergarments were not how she wanted to start her seven-hour trek back to Atlanta. As irritating as it was, at least it took her mind off being back inside a flying metal box.

The elevator door slid open and she raced down the hall. The key was unnecessary as she stood in the open doorway and stared at the bare room she had occupied twenty minutes ago. The sheets had already been stripped and the trash gone. The maid was nowhere to be found. Confused, but out of time to figure it all out, a dejected Tess dragged herself back to the elevator and pushed the button.

"Miss?" A woman's voice called out from behind.

Tess turned around as the elevator dinged.

"Is this what you're looking for?" The maid had mysteriously appeared mid-hall holding up a black leather notebook that looked exactly like her iPad.

Thank goodness she'd come back. She'd have been lost without it, but Tess could have sworn that item was already in her carry-on. She needed to hurry. Ignoring the opening elevator door, Tess trotted over to the maid and opened the case. It wasn't hers. *Weird.* What in the world was going on? She was going to miss her flight with all this foolishness. "Um, thanks, but it's not mine."

Suddenly remembering the elevator, she turned to ask them to hold it, but it was too late. A glimpse of dark hair and a black shirt disappeared behind the pair of large metal doors. The strangest feeling stirred in her gut. She had no words for it, but it felt a lot like loss, a feeling she had unexplainably experienced before. She hastily handed the iPad back to the maid and took slow steps to the elevator. Every detail of the last five minutes played over and over in her head as she waited for the next ride down.

Once free of the elevator, she jogged to the cab, still reeling from the experience and without any answers. Her life had been speckled with enigmatic moments the last few months. They somehow felt important too, like she was on the brink of some grand discovery. What did it all mean?

"Find it?" Warren asked, checking his watch.

"Nope. I'm not even sure what 'it' was," she said as she removed her suit jacket, folded it over her right arm, and then flopped into her seat behind the driver. Tess swiped loose hairs that had fallen from her bun out of her eyes and reached down to pull her bag up onto her lap.

"Guess you'll figure it out when you unpack."

"Mhm." She opened her bag, sifted through a slew of medical conference handouts, and sure enough, at the bottom sat her iPad safe and sound. A heavy sigh slipped out, but not one of relief. This breathy release was full of frustration. The feeling in her gut had remained and she hated not knowing why. Upon further thought, she'd felt off since last night, when she'd had a wicked desire to hit the hotel bar, but being engrossed in the writing of her new research paper, she refused to give in.

Sleep was scarce and scattered between nightmarish flashes from her episode in the mountains and happy, loving scenes of two young women whom she had never met, though she'd been rapt with a familiarity she couldn't describe.

She released her hair from the bun and then fixed it back meticulously. Her attention drifted out the side window to the stream of people on the sidewalk. For some unknown reason, she was compelled to stare at the upcoming corner and the backs of the bystanders waiting to cross. She was unable to tear her eyes away, as if it were the most riveting scene she had ever witnessed.

The brief episodes of her subconsciousness taking control had been increasing in both intensity and frequency as of late. As if a casual spectator to the workings of her own mind, unsettling did not even begin to describe it. Agitating. Disconcerting. Perplexing. All were descriptors that seemed more fitting, but regardless of the chosen adjective, a sense of foreboding accompanied them all.

What was going on? And how could she fix what she didn't understand?

There was nothing remarkable to see. She had been to Seattle several times before, so the sights were familiar. There were a few teenagers engrossed in their cell phones. A tall woman with short graying hair. A nicely dressed gentleman talking on his phone. A woman in a black tank top with a bright bird-looking tattoo on her shoulder blade and medium-length black hair pulled back, faded on the sides.

Tess was drawn to her the most. There was a familiarity about her that couldn't be ignored. Her curiosity refused to quiet. What did she look like? Were her eyes dark or light? Would she be wearing a nice smile or an irritated frown? Would she be the type of woman Tess would take for a drink or one that would never get a second thought?

She was pretty sure they'd at least go for a drink, but the answers would remain a mystery. Tess's cab came to an abrupt halt, jolting her forward and smacking her head on the window. The traffic in front had snarled to a dead stop. Inching forward, her cab opted for an early turn as the mystery woman crossed the street and continued on, leaving her curiosity unfulfilled.

Again, a feeling of loss. Tess sank into her seat, once again confused and profoundly, bewilderingly sad. There had been one other time she had been overcome by such puzzling solemnness— Kansas City. Until this moment, she had forgotten all about it, but that day held so many eerily similar events and emotions—a sort of déjà vu she found unnerving, given her intense response. And that tattoo…

As she compared the two experiences, her phone vibrated with an incoming message. She pulled it from her pocket and groaned. It was Amy.

Can't wait to see you. Have a safe flight. XO

Tess typed out an obligatory response, knowing she would have to listen to it for days if she didn't. *See you soon XO.* The last part left a bitter taste in her mouth. She really did need to put an end to things with Amy soon. She should have done it after the mountain trip, but she'd been too rattled by the memory of the car crash and too cowardly to break Amy's mile-wide smile.

Jeeze, Natalie really could write a paper about her.

"I need a drink," she muttered.

Warren laughed. "Medical conventions do it to me every time."

"Yeah." Tess forced a chuckle. If only the convention was her problem.

CHAPTER FOURTEEN

The elevator settled at the fifth floor with a ding. Tall metal doors opened to the backside view of a female guest in a nicely tailored suit with dark hair up in a tight bun speaking with a maid. Elena's eyes fell to the black and white wingtips. A smile lifted her lips. She worked her way up the tall, lean frame, taking in a shapely backside, then strong shoulders, until she reached the woman's dark hair. There was something about her she couldn't explain. Neither the woman nor the maid, paid them any attention.

A long moment passed and then the doors began to close. Elena's stomach tightened. She was struck with an almost irresistible impulse to reach out and hold the elevator, but why? No one seemed interested in boarding. Still, the woman in the hall had captured her full attention. Elena resisted the urge to bend her body with the receding view to allow a longer look—any extra detail to fuel her imagination, or even a glimpse at her face. What color were her eyes?

It always came back to the eyes.

The doors closed and the elevator moved. Elena shuddered and Marlie took notice. "You okay?"

"Yep."

A brief pause preceded Marlie's next question. "That was a nice suit, huh?"

"It was," Elena dismissively replied.

"And a nice ass."

Elena laughed. "Indeed," she responded with enthusiasm. "And I love a woman bold enough to wear wingtips."

It was Marlie's turn to laugh. "I'll be sure to tell Tracy she needs to give up her heels."

"Please don't," Elena replied with a sigh and a shake of her head. Every now and then, Marlie would still throw Tracy out there. It was exhausting and killed her mood in a big way, though she acknowledged it would linger until she finally dated someone new. Too bad there was no danger of that happening anytime soon.

The bell dinged when they reached their destination. As they made their way through the lobby, Elena's thoughts drifted back to the woman on the fifth floor. The dark hair reminded her of the woman with whom she spent her nights. Would her eyes have been as blue? Were eyes that pure blue and soul-grabbing even possible in real life? Slim chance.

She could hang out in the lobby for a few and possibly get her answer. Marlie would be all for it, if for no other reason than to remind her of it again later. No. What would be the point? Nothing would come of it and she had already given Marlie enough awkward moments to hold over her head until death.

The clear, sunny Seattle morning brought a smile back to Elena's lips as they strolled out of the Waterfront Marriott lobby and started down the street. Grandma would've stayed and waited, claiming some kind of destiny was at work. But she was not Mai.

Determined to put the odd feeling for a stranger from a faraway land behind her, she focused on their day ahead. "We should eat somewhere with a view of Mount Rainier today. The weather is perfect."

"We can do that. I hear Salty's has a fantastic view. Early dinner?"

"Perfect. We can go after my meeting."

"What time you do you think? I can call for a reservation."

"We meet at three, so...anything after five should work."

"Got it."

"I'm nervous."

"Don't be," Marlie said and gave Elena's shoulder a supportive nudge. "The folks at the Burleigh-Green Gallery would be idiots not to give you a show."

"Thank you." Elena smiled and then slowed and threw Marlie a half-hearted scowl. "Ugh. I shouldn't have let you talk me into that extra margarita last night. I feel so sluggish."

"You weren't too hard to convince," Marlie replied through a laugh.

"True," she agreed with a chuckle. "There's just something about drinking at a hotel bar. It feels free and anonymous."

"Perhaps you could have been free to talk up the anonymous hot pant suit had she been there. Maybe we'll try again tonight?"

There was hope in Marlie's words. Hope that spread over to Elena. "Perhaps," Elena said, a small smile working its way up at the thought. A flutter in her belly approved of the idea. Would tonight hold a new opportunity? Could there be a chance to see if the woman was all she had imagined? Was that too much to ask?

Realizing she had fallen into fantasy land, she opted for a return to the present with the subtle distraction of sightseeing, slowing their pace to look out over Elliott Bay as they walked. A red light brought them to a halt and an eerie feeling rushed through Elena, sending the hairs on the back of her neck to full attention for the second time that morning. In the elevator, mere minutes ago, she'd experienced the same phenomenon. She had chalked that one up to the creepy guy beside her leering down her tank top, but now? Looking left, then right over her shoulders, she saw nothing.

"Elena," Marlie called out. "Green means go."

"Sorry," she mumbled, stepping quickly to catch up while still scanning the area for the source of her discomfort. They made it through the intersection and Elena froze five feet beyond the curb. She turned back toward the row of traffic and the yellow cab that had just turned. With great focus, she stared at its rear as if she could see through metal.

"What?" Marlie asked.

"Nothing, I...I don't know. I..." She shook her head. "Nothing, I guess. Sorry."

"Another one of your moments?"

"I uh..." A crease emerged in the center of her forehead as she sought the answer. Yes and No. "This was so much more intense. Like someone watching me. It's probably that solar eclipse."

"That's not until August."

"I know, but the other astrological events that accompany it make this a powerful year in Chinook calendars."

"Then you seriously do need to talk to your grandmother."

"I know. I will."

"I've heard that before. Promise me, Elena."

"Okay, okay. I promise. Happy?"

"I will be if you keep that promise. And if you suddenly become psychic, you need to get me those lottery numbers."

Elena laughed and said, "As if I'd give them to anyone else." She leaned in and bumped Marlie's shoulder with her own. "You're my best friend."

"True, but I had to put it out there."

They shared a smile, then Elena looked back in the direction of the cab. There was definitely something going on with her and she needed to figure it out before she had herself committed. "I will talk to her though. For real this time. That was creepy." She glanced around the block one more time, then looked back at Marlie.

The feeling had passed and the tiny hairs had relaxed their posture. The earlier butterflies in her belly had died, leaving behind a sense of loss she felt to her core. A lingering voice in the back of her mind said there'd be no reason to be at the hotel bar tonight and she couldn't even say why. It was all too much to wrap her head around and all too much like Kansas City.

"Let's get to the market. We'll do the fancy meal tonight, but right now, I'm dying for that lobster grilled cheese." Elena grinned and rubbed her belly.

"You and me both."

"Of all the amazing things you can cook, why haven't you perfected that yet?"

"I don't know. I haven't really tried. And because I'm lazy when it comes to dealing with shellfish and picking out their meat."

Elena laughed. "Fair enough. What if I did it?"

"If you actually did anything in the preparation of food, I'd say we need to have a party."

"Very funny." She nudged her friend. "Also, very true." Resisting the urge to take one more look around, Elena forced a smile and continued on her way. The weirdness was beginning to get out of hand.

CHAPTER FIFTEEN

Present Day - July 9, 2017

Atlanta

Tess lay unconscious in her hospital bed, oblivious to the doctor checking her vitals or her brother's nervous pacing. While her bruised and battered body remained still, her mind came alive with the most vivid of dreams. No scattered pictures of the weird or random. No flashes of obscurity. This was perfect scene by scene, full color, complete with temperature and sensations, as if a cherished old memory was replaying in her head.

She hovered above two young girls in another time and place, familiar enough to tickle the synapses of her hippocampus, yet not at all enough to fire and say, "A ha! I know them!" The cool air pricked her skin, but the sight of the two girls in a canoe smiling at one another warmed her soul. Her presence unnoticed, she moved closer, listening in on their conversation.

"Abbie, stop being such a tease and paddle. It's getting chilly."

"Sorry, my love, but I know how to warm you up." Abbie, the blonde, slid closer and draped her arm around the redhead's waist.

"Yes, you do," the redhead agreed with a lopsided grin. The thin white dress she was wearing did little to hide the cold. "But not in the middle of the lake. Anyone could see us." She removed the hand with tender care and shot Abbie an annoyed glance, though her body betrayed her words as she scooted as close as clothes allowed.

Tess floated closer still, until her body became one with Abbie's. She could hear every thought and feel the pounding of the girl's heart as if it were her own. The most profound of all the sensations bombarding her, however, was something she'd never felt before—wholeness. The love coursing through her body for the redhead, Mary, filled the empty space that had resided in her chest every day of her thirty-seven years. Tess was quickly enraptured by the new emotion, allowing herself to become fully immersed with Abbie so as not to miss one single bit of the experience.

There weren't many things Abbie loved more than making Mary blush. Pale, creamy skin would turn the most wonderful pink shade and vibrant, deep brown eyes sparkled in a way that was only ever meant for her. She leaned in close, dropping her voice an octave when she asked, "Would that be so bad?"

Her lover shivered and leaned in just enough to brush their cheeks together in a sign of affection before pulling away. "You know how people are here. We can't." The sparkle dimmed and Mary turned her head, using her unruly, long red curls to hide her face.

The warmth of Mary's hand covered Abbie's, but the refusal left her cold. She wasn't surprised. It was the third time she had asked and the third time she had been denied. Each time hurt more than the last. They had shared their passions behind closed doors, but in the open, Mary's fears kept winning out.

Why couldn't Mary be brave? Fight for love?

"But I love you. I don't care who knows." Abbie desperately hoped to convince Mary to leave and make a life together. She knew she could make Mary the happiest woman on earth, given the chance.

"I love you too, but my parents…and George…and our friends."

"I only care about you, Mary. About us. We should leave together, start a life somewhere else. Maybe a big city, like New York?" Abbie glanced over the side of the row boat and stared at her reflection in the water's surface—short, unkempt blonde hair, bright blue eyes, and a boyish button-down shirt. Mary was so feminine in her dress and dolled-up hair, but Abbie…she was who she was, comfortably so. Was that what made Mary so afraid?

"I don't know. Would you really leave our fam-" Mary's demure voice faded away. Her lips continued to move, but didn't match the words filling Abbie's ears.

"Any change, Doctor?"

"Her vitals are stronger and there's been brain activity similar to that of dreaming, so that's encouraging."

Mary's beautiful face slowly dissipated, taking a piece of Abbie's heart and soul with each faded feature. Gone was her smile, her button nose, and the warmest brown eyes ever put on this Earth. The loss left a weight as heavy as a hippo sitting square on her chest, crushing her lungs, holding her breath hostage. A sliver of blinding light erased the last remains of Mary's form, leaving Abbie alone to bear the burden of the suffocating emptiness within her.

"So, there is hope then?"

"We won't know anything for certain until she wakes up, but...I am cautiously optimistic."

Tess cracked open an eye only to be blinded by horrible fluorescent lighting that forced her back into the darkness. She squeezed her lids shut tight. An agonizing pain shot through her skull. The voices around her were familiar, though she lacked the ability to place names or faces. The incessant chorus of rhythmic beeps made her want to gouge out her eardrums as they echoed into the depths of her aching head.

Beeping? Strange voices?

Unable to think about a second attempt at opening her eyes, she tried to speak, finding it harder than she remembered to form a coherent thought, much less physically form a word. Her throat was dry. Her tongue failed to obey. Her brain couldn't seem to put her question into physical form. Most of all, she couldn't catch a full breath.

"Wh—? Wh—?" A much-needed gasp of air filled her lungs, when moments ago she'd thought they had filled for the final time.

"Tess? Oh my god! Tess! Doctor! She's awake!" A woman's high-pitched voice reverberated off the walls.

The shrill screech was like a million razors on her brain that sliced every neuron and caused her to shrivel in pain. Tess groaned her discomfort and the voice finally hushed, though it continued to ramble in the distance.

"Shhh, it's okay, Tess. You're okay," a man soothed. Once again, familiarity poked at her memory, but she couldn't grab ahold of the answer.

Her eyes still closed, her bearings still not gotten, she whispered, "Where...?"

"You're in the hospital. You had a terrible accident." A gentle hand brushed her forehead. "It's me, Evan, your brother. You're going to be okay, Tess."

Squeezing her eyes shut tighter, her mind tumbled out of control. Nothing made sense. Her head ached. Her body throbbed in pain. She had so many questions, like who the heck was Evan?

Her eyes fought to open and locked briefly with his. No recognition flashed. Frustration welled inside. The next question was even more important, because it directly involved her. She prayed the result would be better than the first. But she had to hurry. Fatigue was making a swift claim to her body.

Fading fast, she willed her brain and tongue to function as one. "Who's Tess?" she mumbled and then she was out cold once again.

∞ ∞ ∞

"How long will the amnesia last?" Amy asked.

Evan slipped his arm over her shoulder as he stared at his sister resting peacefully. She had drifted back to sleep moments after waking. The cuts, bruises, and bandages were all a blatant reminder he should be more excited she had woken up at all, but her quick return to unconsciousness had stolen his joy and left fear in its wake.

"It's difficult to tell," Dr. Coleman said. "She sustained a severe trauma to the brain. We're lucky she's even awake at all, though she may be out again for a while. It's not unusual for them to stay in a coma longer than seven days as the brain heals. I'll take her down shortly for another scan."

"Thank you, Doctor," Amy and Evan said in unison.

The doctor offered a sympathetic smile before leaving the room.

"We'll just have to be patient. You know how Tess is, she's a pain in the ass," Evan laughed, but Amy cried.

"What? What's wrong?" In a panic, he faced her and sought to meet her eyes.

"She is a pain in the ass and she can be so thoughtless, but I love her."

"I know you do. You're here. She'll be happy to see you."

"No. No, she won't." Amy shook her head and sucked in a breath. "That morning…the day of the accident…she left me a breakup note by the bed. We had an argument on the phone. I was so pissed at her. My heart was broken, or at least I thought it was. It couldn't compare to how broken it felt when you called and told me about the accident. Deep down, I hoped we could talk it out, that I could get her to let go and let me in."

"Oh, Amy. I'm so sorry." Evan enveloped her in a consoling hug.

Amy buried her face in his shoulder, accepting the comfort, then had a change of heart. Her head shook in steadfast refusal and she tried to push away. "No, I'm sorry. I should probably go. I have no right to be here."

Evan held strong, but pulled back enough to look her in the eye. "You have every right. You love her and you've been by her side all week. I know Tess has a horrible track record in relationships and I'm sorry she hurt you, but please stay. Maybe this will be a wake-up call for her. I can't promise it will end any differently, but if you still want her, then stay. Fight for her."

"I do," she sniffled. "I will. Thank you, Evan." Amy finally gave in and reciprocated his hug.

"Mary?" Tess called out in her delirium.

"Who's Mary?" Evan asked in a whisper.

Amy shrugged, but struggled to hide the hurt in her eyes at hearing another woman's name fall from Tess's lips. She pulled herself free and walked to the bed. Caution filled every step. Taking Tess's hand in hers, she stroked the pale, cold skin softly with her thumb and asked, "Who's Mary?"

No answer.

Amy reached up and ran her hand over long dark hair. "Tess, honey, who is Mary?"

"Mary? Where are you, my love?"

Amy froze.

Evan looked on in proverbial slow motion as Amy's face dropped, her painful expression signifying the very moment her heart had shattered into pieces. He rushed to her side, catching her before her crumbling knees sent her to the hard, linoleum floor. "Amy. She doesn't know what she's saying. She doesn't even know who she is."

"That may be, but she's never called me 'Love.'" She politely, but firmly removed his grasp, then steadied her legs and straightened her shirt. With as much dignity as she could muster, she took one more look at her ex-girlfriend and then grabbed her keys and headed for the door.

"Amy…"

"I can't right now, Evan. Let me know if you need anything and please tell me when she wakes up. I umm…I need some time."

Nodding, he turned his attention back to his sister. Tess shifted uncomfortably in her bed and murmured incoherent words. Evan shook his head. He'd thought he had known most everything about his sister, except the unexplainable reason she could never seem to love anyone outside of her family. Who could this mystery woman be and why hadn't he met her? He stepped closer, leaned in, and repeated Amy's question. "Who is Mary?"

No reply came. Tess was asleep and no answers would be had today, if ever. Brain trauma manifested itself in so many ways. His bigger concern was her amnesia. Evan scooted a chair to her side and sat down. He took her hand in his and sent prayers for a quick and healthy return. They would take the rest one step at a time.

CHAPTER SIXTEEN

Portland - Same Day

"So, you've seen this woman in your dreams?" Mai asked as she settled back on the couch and stared at Elena expectantly. The worn, old sofa was covered in colorful hand-woven blankets—gifts from friends and loved ones throughout the years.

Elena paused before answering. Her gaze left Mai and traveled about the room. The red cedar walls of the old cabin she'd spent so much time in as a child surrounded her, warmed her, grounded her, bringing normalcy to the very abnormal conversation they were about to have. She circled back until her eyes met Mai's patient gaze. It all sounded so crazy, but she knew her grandmother would be the last one to think so. She believed in spirits, energy, and all things supernatural. "Yes."

"Even before the hospital?" Mai inquired.

"Mhm. For years now."

"When did it start?"

Mai's curiosity had been tickled. The sparkle of excitement shone in her eyes from the thrill of the search and

Elena knew her grandmother would be a very busy lady until an answer had been found.

"I don't know exactly. When I was a girl, not long after cancer took Mom away. At first, I thought she was like a guardian angel, but Dad was a man of science and insisted it was my way of dealing with tragedy. I never believed him. It felt too personal. After a while, I just kept it to myself. Then..." She shifted in her spot. Her fidgety fingers needed to be silenced, so Elena locked them together and set them on her lap.

She was grateful Mai had remained quiet, allowing her to form her thoughts and voice them without interruption. After a long breath, she continued, "After my Dad passed, there were a few days with no dreams at all. It was weird how sad and lonely that loss made me feel. I loved my father of course, but losing her...it was like I'd lost a piece of me." The ache of the painful memory made her pause to gather herself.

"She returned, thankfully, and the dreams have evolved as I've aged. They've actually been more intense since you gave me the dreamcatcher." She leaned back with a breathy sigh of relief, happy to have it all off her chest. She'd never told anyone about her younger years, not even Marlie.

"Why have you never mentioned it?"

"I meant to," she responded softly like a scared child issuing a confession. "I was supposed to. I even promised Marlie, but..." she trailed off and looked away. It was embarrassing to admit such a thing to anyone, much less herself.

Understanding her apprehension, as she always did so well, Mai moved past the confession and said, "Well, you're here now, so let's try to get some answers."

Elena nodded and offered her grandmother a soft, appreciative smile. She was thankful for the lack of judgement regarding her predicament, as well as the decision not to lecture her need to hide.

Always one to consider her options, Mai took a minute to think before she asked, "Does she make you feel afraid of her?"

"No. Quite the opposite." A giant grin took shape, one Elena couldn't stop if she tried. "I find comfort in her. So much so, that it pains me to leave her when I wake."

Mai smiled in return. "Does she urge you to make bad choices?"

Not unless trying to have sex in a canoe in the middle of a lake was a bad choice. Elena smiled coyly, blushing when her grandma raised an inquisitive brow. "Never." She cleared her throat and shifted before continuing, "We do random things like canoe, or walk, or picnic under a tree beside the water. It's just, I feel so present. It feels every bit as real as sitting here with you."

"Is she a blurry figure or clear as day?"

"I can tell you every line, every freckle, even the little mole above her left eyebrow."

"Interesting."

"Why is that?"

"Well, often we have a spirit guide, a being that helps us in sleep to handle stress, big life decisions, or subconscious concerns. They take many forms—a person, an animal, a disguise. They can change according to our level of comfort and understanding. Other times, you have a dream of someone you've met that holds a significance to you, known or unknown, and they can be seen more clearly because you have seen them in the flesh. Typically, when you dream of a stranger, erotic or otherwise, their face is unclear, leaving it open for your own interpretation, but for it to be someone you've never met and to have such a clear view is unusual."

"So, I *am* crazy." Elena buried her face in her hands and groaned loudly.

"Not at all, my dear." Mai chuckled and placed her hand on Elena's knee. "Give me a moment." She stood and walked to the back wall of the room. Its surface was lined with homemade shelves that created a vast bookcase stretching from end to end of its twenty-foot expanse. Her fingers traipsed across a seemingly endless selection of books, all either tribal, metaphysical, or spiritual in nature.

"Given the lunar eclipse," she began while still in search of her desired read, "Mercury retrograde, solar eclipse trifecta this August, it's no surprise your visions have increased. It brings a very powerful energy shift. Even more so for you since..." she trailed off as she considered the titles before her.

"I'd read about that." She'd mentioned it to Marlie, but how much role could it really play? Curiosity burned within. Elena hung on every breath as she awaited the reasoning behind Mai's thought process. Ten long seconds had passed and no answer had come. Mai had opened one book, fingered through several pages, then put it back and continued her search, but offered no more explanation. Elena could take the silence no longer. She had to know what her grandmother was thinking. "Since what?"

No answer. Her grandmother was on a mission and currently oblivious to her presence.

"Mai?" she called again a little louder.

"Hmm?" Mai glanced over her shoulder. Her questioning eyes revealed she had forgotten her previous statement.

"Since what?" Elena repeated. Her frustration plain as day in the tone of her voice.

"I'm sorry, dear…what were we talking about?" Mai asked innocently, their earlier conversation a victim of her overactive mind.

Elena sighed and shook her head. "You mentioned some trifecta and how it would affect me more than others. Why?"

"Oh that," Mai said with a hint of a laugh. "Because you were conceived during a total solar eclipse that occurred right overhead." Mai paused when she reached an old book with a worn brown jacket. "Plus, you've got powerful Chinook blood in you."

She pulled it out with care and fingered gently through the pages. "Hmm. Ah. Mhm."

"What's it say?"

"Hold yer horses." Mai skimmed further down the page. "Very interesting indeed."

"Grandma," Elena whined.

"Okay, but before I tell you, I have to test my hypothesis."

Elena frowned. She'd prefer to hear this hypothesis up front, but past experience proved her grandmother wouldn't budge. When it came to matters of the spirit world, Mai had always been steadfast in her approach.

"Fine," Elena huffed and crossed her arms, looking every bit the pouting child she had been years ago when her grandmother would tell her no.

Mai disappeared into the basement and returned minutes later with another book, a clove of sage, and some incense. She set them on an old red cedar table her late husband, Grandpa Cody, had made. Mai only used it on special occasions. The legs were adorned with carvings of various animals—a blue jay, an owl, a salmon, and a coyote.

Never having witnessed such a ritual, Elena watched with skepticism, but said nothing. Once set up—the incense burning in the doorway, the sage aflame with two stones on either side atop the table, and the book opened to a specific passage—Mai looked up at her granddaughter and smiled.

"Are you going to tell me now?" Elena's knee bounced in rapid succession serving as a release for her anxious energy.

"After." Mai paid her impatience no mind. "First, I want to look at your spirit. I have to see who is surrounding you, and make sure you are clear. Sit here, please," she said and motioned to the floor in front of her.

"Okayyy…" Elena hesitantly slid from her spot on the couch and arranged herself near her grandmother's feet as Mai began to speak in Native American tongue. Not as fluent as she should be in Chinook, she did make out a few words, including the word "spirit guide." Mai fell silent and Elena searched the room for signs that anything at all was happening.

Nothing. Not a sound or a breeze or even a movement from Mai. What had she expected anyway? Levitating objects? Ghostly appearances? Possession?

Silly.

She stared up at her grandmother awaiting her next direction, if any, to come. Her nervousness mixed with hopefulness. She needed answers. If they didn't come here, then she very well could be crazy.

∞ ∞ ∞

Reaching down, Mai's eyes closed as she placed a hand on Elena's shoulder. "I see the bear is very protective of you. You have a beautiful aura. Warm, full of life, and…"

"And what?"

"It...it's not clear..." A long pause filled the room with silence before she spoke again. "Ahhh...hello, dear," she greeted a new visitor. "Come closer. I won't hurt you." The most welcoming of smiles graced Mai's lips as she reached her left hand out, her eyes still closed.

"Huh?" A confused Elena asked, not being privy to her vision.

"It's two young girls, hand in hand. One's energy is connected to yours. The other's..." Mai trailed off again as she examined the vision that had appeared before her. "It goes into the distance. I can't see them clearly, but they are very close. Their auras are interwoven."

The light, such beautiful, warm light emanating unconditional love enveloped Mai, bringing with it a feeling of belonging and peace. The souls were accepting of her presence. Mai smiled. While she had always known her granddaughter was special, she had never imagined something so rare and powerful. This was something she had only read in books, been told in ancient lore, and while she had always believed the phenomenon to be true, had never had the chance to bear witness. Until now. But without previous experience, she had to be sure, dead sure, before she spoke the words aloud.

"Elena, I need you to picture this woman you dream of. Close your eyes and concentrate on her face as if she were with you right now."

Elena shut her eyes and did as she was told.

Slowly, the young girl connected to Elena faded into the background right before Mai's eyes. The remaining figure came closer, however, her aura remained joined to the other's in a pinpoint of light in the distance. Mai waved the girl closer, but despite great effort, she couldn't seem to make the approach. Waves of sadness and pleading crashed against Mai. The light in the distance grew nearer, blinding Mai, though the figure remained still.

"Concentrate harder, Elena, please."

"I'll try, but I...I'm so tired."

Mai focused all her energy on fighting through the light. Her pained eyes squinted despite being closed. The vague form of a girl soon morphed into a woman, her face detailed as clear as day as she stood in disbelief and awe. A river of dark navy-colored energy outlined her form amid the white surroundings. "She has dark hair and kind blue eyes, but there is a coldness surrounding her. Not one of evil or wrong doing, but...she is alone. Lost. Searching. Her heart is unable to be full."

The light began to dim. "Stay with me," Mai urged both Elena and the spirit.

With a gasp, Elena collapsed forward. The dark-haired woman in the vision fell to her knees. Her head dropped in resignation, then she vanished, sending the vision into darkness.

Mai fell back on the couch, feeling the loss as if it were her own. "Amazing," she breathed out. Slowly, she returned to reality and the sight of her granddaughter slumped over on the floor.

Panic set in. Had it been too much for Elena? She needed to check on her granddaughter, but her old body, sapped of strength, refused to allow movement. All she could muster was the energy to speak. "Elena, are you okay?" Her voice was as weak as her deadened limbs.

"Yeah. Just exhausted." A heavy breath followed Elena's words. She remained motionless. "That was...I've never experienced anything like that before."

Mai sighed in relief. She didn't dare move a muscle other than the ones needed for a slow smile to crawl up her lips. The worry in her eyes shifted to glorious revelation. "Remember the trifecta I mentioned?"

"Mhm," Elena mumbled, sounding as drained as Mai despite her youth.

"Well, some souls are more sensitive than others to that energy shift, especially when they're separated from their other half. There are many views on the topic. Our culture certainly has its own ideas about the afterlife, but there are others who believe that some souls are connected throughout many lives, sometimes enjoying a reunion, other times not. Eclipses are a time for change and this trifecta is an opportunity for the universe to play cupid, so to speak, giving the souls a push to form their union." Her smile grew brighter.

"You, my dear Elena, are most certainly connected." Mai's words sparkled with the awe of great possibility. "It was beautiful and powerful. The universe is taking action. This is your chance, or you may lose it for the rest of this lifetime."

Finally mustering the strength to roll onto her back, Elena met her grandmother's excited gaze. Her eyes narrowed in disbelieving suspicion while flashing a million questions through her concentrated stare. "So, you're saying…?"

"You, my dear Elena, have a soul mate. And whether she knows it or not, she is desperate to find you."

CHAPTER SEVENTEEN

Atlanta - July 10, 2017

The rhythmic beep of Tess's heart monitor picked up its pace as she stirred in her bed. Her eyelids fluttered, the rapid movements beneath them a result of her peak dream state. Once again, the scene had a familiar feel. The connection ran deep enough to warrant an emotional response, but unlike the happy one from earlier, this one left a gripping discomfort in her chest. An uncomfortable whimper welled in her throat. Her head tossed to the right. The fight to wake up had begun, but her subconscious had other plans.

Tall trees lined the rolling hills surrounding her. The late morning sky had a patch of blue that was quickly being swallowed by ominous-looking clouds. Sitting at the end of a road in an old, red, 1941 Chevy farm truck, she gripped a cedar carved owl tight in her hands—hands with uneven nails and calluses. She looked in the rearview mirror and stared at the reflection of a round face topped with short, messy blonde hair. The edges of her memory believed her hair to be dark and her face more angled, but her blue eyes were perfectly familiar.

Her attention was drawn out the window to the little white Baptist church surrounded by cars. Yellow and white roses decorated the entrance. A bout of dizziness struck as the details of the life changing day rushed to the forefront—Mary was getting married.

She scoffed. Mary had always hated roses, but it was still the perfect picture of happiness, far from the feeling welling inside of her. The nauseating rolling in her stomach grew as the last of the guests were being ushered inside. Soon, Mary would no longer be hers.

Though she had intended to be the maid of honor, she couldn't bear to attend the ceremony and had stepped down, much to Mary's discontent. As far as she was concerned, this day would forever be known as a day of loss. If she were a wealthy woman, she would buy a headstone—the birthdate being the day they had met and Mary's wedding, the day her heart withered and died—and she would have it placed under their tree in the forest.

In time, other lovers would find it, perhaps searching for their own perfect spot as they imagined a life together. They would ponder the story of its existence, oblivious to its mockery of dreams they hold dear. Being broke, however, she would settle for marking the date in black on her calendar until the end of her days.

The arrival of the dark, stormy clouds matched her mood. Her head fell to the steering wheel. The sorrow and loss of her true love squeezed her chest to the point of breathless heaves as tears rolled down her cheeks. The faint sound of "Here Comes the Bride" was the final straw. She cranked the engine as the rain began to fall, as if the heavens had offered a show of their sympathy for her predicament.

She leaned over, yanked open the glove box, shoved the owl inside, and then slammed it shut with such force the panel creaked under the pressure. Shifting the truck into drive, she cruised slowly past the church entrance. She didn't dare look inside.

A light blue Cadillac convertible with strings of cans tied to the back and a "Just Married" sign was too much to bear. At least the rain would keep them from enjoying the magic of driving with the top down, a small consolation given her loss. She wiped her eyes as she sped up, determined to leave that little town and her broken heart in the rearview mirror.

"Abbie! Abigail!"

The sweet sound of her name called from Mary's lips had her foot instantly on the brake. She glanced back to find her love running through the rain at full speed, heels tossed aside and white dress high in her hands.

An uncontrollable smile shone like the sun breaking through a storm as she reached across and flung the door open.

Mary was hardly inside when her jilted groom, George, came bolting out after her.

"Drive!" Mary screeched. "Drive, Abbie!"

Pedal to the floor, she tore away as they laughed, giddy with joy and relief.

"I couldn't do it. I couldn't marry him. I love you, Abigail."

Her heart full, her smile luminous, Abbie reached across and joined their hands. "I love you too, Mary. You're my light, my love." She kissed Mary's hand. "Where to?"

"Anywhere, as long as I'm with you."

They sped along the twisty country roads. The rain eased slightly, bringing a sense that all was well in the world. For several beautiful minutes it was, until the light blue Cadillac convertible appeared in the rearview mirror, hot on their tail.

"George," she muttered and accelerated.

"Be careful, Abbie." Mary dug a set of manicured nails into Abbie's denim clad thigh.

With eyes firm on the road and her grip secure on the wheel, she replied with confidence, "I will." And she meant it with every fiber in her being. They were never going back to that damned town.

George closed in on them, flashing his lights and yelling out his window for them to pull over, but she would have none of it. She took the curve hard, throwing Mary into the door with a yelp. "Sorry," she said, though her gaze never wavered and her intent remained unchanged.

"Maybe we should-"

"No!"

The rain began again, pounding the truck with a fierceness that matched her determination.

"Please slow down, Abbie," Mary pleaded, her voice trembling. Her hands latched onto the door and dash, anchoring her during the rough ride. Mary screamed when the back end of the truck fishtailed.

"I got it," Abbie said and quickly righted their path.

George honked his horn again, refusing to let them escape. The S curve ahead did nothing to slow either's pace as they raced at breakneck speeds.

CRACK!

THUD!

A tree limb crashed to the ground in front of them and Abbie swerved to miss it. She was powerless to control their path. Their truck skittered onto two wheels. A shrill scream filled the cab as they took out the Route 441 sign. Their truck soared over the ledge and plummeted down the embankment, rolling violently until it reached the bottom in a crumbled heap.

Barely conscious, George's screams from above were ignored. She stretched her trembling arm out to Mary. Unable to cross the full distance, she covered Mary's limp and bloodied hand with her own in the middle of the seat. "I'm sorry. I love you."

A weak groan was her only response. No forgiveness. No "I love you too." No "it'll be okay." Only the sound of pain. She had managed to hurt the one person she loved most. The one person she would sacrifice herself for. She had caused this. Her recklessness, her pride, her ego. She didn't deserve Mary.

Guilt swallowed her whole, grabbing a hold of her heart and crumbling it to bits, sending an ache so deep, so widespread, that breathing became impossible. In the deafening silence, she bargained her life for Mary's to the heavens over and over until the slowing beat of her heart and the lessening intake of breath forced daylight to succumb to darkness.

Tess bolted upright in bed, gasping and heaving, sucking in as much air as she could to restore the life she'd thought she lost. The light too bright to handle, she covered her face with her hands and sobbed. Tears streaked her cheeks. A squeezing pain spread through her chest and radiated down both arms. Dizziness set in and her stomach turned. It was worse than the hangover after that homemade moonshine last summer. The memory of the crash and Mary's bloodied hand sent bile into her throat. She welcomed the discomfort. She deserved it, and far worse.

What have I done? Mary...I hurt Mary. Where is she? I have to see her. I have to apologize. She has to be okay. I'll never forgive myself if-

Piercing pain ripped through her left temple when a high-pitched beep repeatedly echoed throughout the room.

Dad gummed beeping! Make it stop!

Her fingers parted slightly, controlling the amount of light hitting her pupils as she peeked at her surroundings. Sterile white walls. Curtains. A man at the foot of her bed with a clipboard in hand, a stethoscope around his neck, and a long white coat tailored to his lanky frame. His curious gaze observed her every action.

A doctor? Where am I?

"Hello, I'm Doctor Coleman. How are you feeling today?" He stepped around to the side of her bed and silenced the agonizing beep.

"Sore. Confused. Where's Mary?" A gentle southern accent danced through her words.

"Mary?" The doctor scribbled something quickly, then looked back up and awaited her response.

She picked up on his blank stare and questioning tone, causing her to second guess the events flashing through her mind that made her sick beyond belief. "Yes, Mary. We were driving in the storm and..." Words slipped away and her lungs failed. The memory was brutal enough, but saying it aloud...words had the ability to create realities. *Please let it just be a nightmare.* She gulped for breath. Wide blue eyes darted around the room.

"And then what?" he prodded.

"I uh, lost control of my truck. We went off the cliff." She stopped abruptly. Reliving the moment was more than she could stand. Again, a wave of dread struck, crashing as hard as a twenty-foot wave rolling her violently through its white wash. Had she been standing, she would have collapsed.

"Where's Mary?" Her voice cracked. The tears returned. She gripped her hands into tight fists, balling them into the sheets to keep her shaking at bay. "Is she okay? I...I have to see her. I gotta tell her I'm sorry. It was all my fault." Tess threw the blankets from her legs and attempted to get out of bed.

Dr. Coleman stepped up and stopped her with a hand to the chest and a shake of his head.

"But I have to see her. I have to know if I hurt her." Her desperation was clear.

He softened as sympathy etched its way onto his expression. "You can see her when we get you back on your feet."

"But I'm good now. See?" A second attempt was made to leave the bed, but he held her in place.

"I must insist you stay in bed. You're too unstable to be on your feet, but we'll get you there. Be patient." The doctor began a series of checks that included her pupils and tracking. "Your last scans looked good," he explained as he worked. "We'll keep you here a bit for monitoring to make sure there are no surprises and begin rehab for your brain trauma."

"But what if...when I...she..." Patience had gone extinct. Mary trumped all reasonable thought.

"Relax, please." He took ahold of her right hand and looked her in the eye to draw her full attention. "I can tell you that you did *not* drive off a cliff, you-"

"What?" she interrupted. A swell of hope rippled in her chest.

"No cliffs, but you *were* hit by a truck."

"I was hit?" Tess repeated. "By a truck?" She searched high and low for any recollection, but came up empty. The lack of memory was disturbing and confusing, but she was relieved the ugly events in her mind had been just that— all in her mind. Now, if she could get them out of her mind. She shook her head and blew out a heavy breath. Her body sagged and fatigue set in quickly, the anxiety and her weakened state taking its toll.

Dr. Coleman released her hand and steadied her. "That's right, but head trauma can do that to you. Memory lapses, distorted memories, headaches, sensitivity to light, nausea, and much more. In your case, we'll have to wait and see, but you're very lucky to be alive."

"Not feeling very lucky at the moment."

A light chuckle fell out of the doctor. "I understand."

"So, it was only a dream then? Mary's fine?"

"Yes, although I don't know anything about anyone named Mary. You were alone when they brought you in." He helped her settle back in and then pulled the blankets up to her chest.

Tess nodded. The weight had lifted, but the urgency was still there. Mary made everything better. "Can I call her? I really have to talk to her."

"I'll see what I can do, but I really need you to rest. Your brother and Amy have been in to see you. They've been very worried. I'll let them know you're awake."

Tess nodded again, brushing aside the fact she had no clue who Amy was, but assumed her to be her brother's girlfriend. The only thing Kenny went through faster than women was beer.

"What about my parents?"

"I'm sorry, I haven't seen them."

He offered a warm smile that Tess returned, but it was half-hearted. Her mom and dad had become cold and distant as her love for Mary had been undeterred by their efforts to sway her. Not even the fear of God could change the person her heart and soul burned for and she was fine with that.

They, however, were ashamed and quite vocal about it. One thing was for sure, if the accident had been an attempt at divine intervention to right her sinning ways, God had failed. If anything, it had solidified her feelings. Mary was the only one for her and as soon as she was free of this place, she would find a way for them to be together.

"Before I go," Dr. Coleman interrupted her thoughts. "I'm going to ask you a couple of questions. Just simple ones to get your brain going. I know it's early, but I have to get a baseline for your recovery," he explained with a gentle smile.

His demeanor set her at ease, and while all she wanted to do was talk to Mary, she relaxed into the bed, feeling sleep calling her name again. "All right."

"What's your name?"

"Abigail Carter."

He paused, made a note, then asked, "What year is it?"

"Nineteen fifty-four."

"What city and state do you live in?"

"Bryson City, North Carolina."

Another note was made on the chart and then he looked up and smiled warmly once more. "I'll be back to check on you again later."

She gave him a nod and watched with heavy lids as he left the room. The television sure looked a lot different than the one at her house, but they probably had fancier ones in the hospitals. The two times she had visited one, they'd had all kinds of machines and gadgets that boggled her mind. Rather than contemplate the wonders of science and technology, her thoughts drifted to Mary and when she might see her again, until sleep took hold once more.

CHAPTER EIGHTEEN

The next couple of days were much the same. Doctors and nurses came and went, checking vitals and asking random questions. Tess was feeling better, despite a lingering headache, so her impatience was on the rise. Today she would be allowed to walk the hall with a nurse in tow. Being cooped up had never sat well with her. She was a mover and all she had been able to think about during her downtime was why Mary hadn't come to visit, except in her dreams.

It's all that George's fault. I know it is.

"You ready for your walk?" Nurse Barbara asked with a warm smile. The short, stocky older woman was always full of cheer.

"Yes, Ma'am. Been looking forward to it all morning."

Barbara helped her from the bed and allowed her to get her bearings before letting go. "Any dizziness?"

"No."

"Good. Now take your time and if you feel woozy, let me know." Barbara tied the back of the gown shut and placed a blanket over Tess's shoulders.

Tess took small steps. It felt good to stretch her legs. The long days of lying around had her stiff and sore all over. A proud grin crossed her lips and Barbara patted her on the back as they reached the end of the hall.

"How do you feel?"

"Tired, but okay. I hate this cast though." She scratched at the edges of the plaster encasing her left arm.

Barbara chuckled. "Everyone does. Do you need a rest before we head back?"

"No. I think I can make it. I gotta get strong so I can find Mary."

Barbara offered a smile, though not as bright as her usual ones. Tess paid it no mind and they made a slow turn to head back down the hall. As she walked through her doorway, Tess grinned again. She had hit her goal. *Victory!*

She let out an exhausted breath and turned to Barbara to celebrate. Without warning, her knees grew weak. The room spun. She opened her mouth to speak, but no words came out as she crumbled into the nurse's arms.

∞ ∞ ∞

Barbara quickly lowered Tess's limp body safely to the floor and then ran to the help button, pressing it repeatedly as Tess began to convulse. The seizure clenched every muscle in her body to its breaking point. Barbara grabbed a pillow and slipped it under Tess's head to prevent more trauma, but knowing better than to get in the way, she turned her focus to making sure the area was clear of anything Tess could possibly hit. Content that she had done her best, she rushed into the hallway to meet the nurse in charge, Doris.

After a quick assessment of the situation, Doris paged the doctor on call. She picked up Tess's chart and scanned the notes, then added a new one of her own. "What happened?"

"We went for her therapy walk," Barbara explained in a breathless ramble. "She was fine. She did really well, actually. Then, she just collapsed." She stared back helplessly as Tess's limp form repeatedly stiffened and jerked.

"You did fine, Barbara. There was nothing else you could do. All we can do now is wait."

∞ ∞ ∞

July 14, 2017

The damned fluorescent lights pierced her eyes like knives. Tess cursed as she struggled to assess her surroundings. She was alone, soothed by the gentle monotone beep of her heart monitor.

A cast wrapped her left forearm. Bandages covered her right shoulder. Lifting her right arm was a problem and there was nothing but pain whenever she tried to move any muscle at all. Her body was spent, like the one time she had tried to run a marathon. That was a day she really thought she was going to die. Good lord, had she tried to run another one?

Nope. There was a cast. And bandages. Casts and bandages were a bad sign. *What happened to me?*

An orderly rushed past her room in a flash. A nurse sped by headed the other direction. The longer she watched, the more intricate the symphony of steps, beeps, and voices until she had lulled herself back to sleep.

Hours later, she awoke to the soft sounds of the nurse checking her vitals and changing her bag of saline solution. Her mouth was bone dry and her attempt at speaking rendered her unable to muster much more than a cough. The nurse smiled softly and passed her a cup of water. Tess downed several gulps far too quickly and then gasped for a breath. "Thank you," she choked out.

"Take it easy. How are you feeling?" The young nurse whose badge read "Annie" took her cup. She refilled it, then set it aside and stared expectantly in wait of a response.

Tess shrugged. "Well as can be, I guess. What happened?" Her words noticeably lacked the slight southern twang that had graced them the last few days.

Annie paused, studying her curiously before answering, "You had a little seizure. A residual from your injury."

"What was my injury?"

Annie's response was a perplexed expression that left Tess with more questions. "I'll let the doctor tell you." Without any further explanation, Annie rushed out of the room.

Tess didn't have to wait long as Dr. Coleman returned with a bright smile. "You gave us quite the scare, but I think you're through the worst now."

"What happened to me? How long have I been here? What's my diagnosis?" Tess launched a barrage of questions.

His left brow rose at the change in both demeanor and accent. "I'll answer your questions in a moment. First, I have few for you. What is your name?"

"Doctor Contessa Kenner."

"Good. What year is it?"

Knowing the routine, Tess sped up the question portion of their conversation by spurting the required answers in succession. "Twenty-seventeen. We're in Atlanta, Georgia. And unless it's the result of my accident playing with my memories, our President is Donald Trump."

"No, that's real." He laughed and typed on his tablet. "You were hit by a truck and brought into our E.R. with severe head trauma. You also broke both your left radius and ulna. Yesterday you collapsed during a walk due to a brain hemorrhage, but we repaired the bleeder in your temporal lobe. Time and rest are what you need now. Do you remember any of that?"

"No." She scratched at her cast.

"That's not unusual, given the severity of your injuries. Tess, do you know anyone named Mary?"

"Umm...no. Not that I recall. Should I?"

"Not necessarily." He ignored her questioning stare and pushed on. "What about Evan?

"Yes, he's my little brother, the tech guru." A proud smile appeared.

"And what about Amy?"

"Was she here? Oh god." A look of horror contorted her face.

"I'll take that as a yes."

"How long have I been here?"

"About two weeks."

"Two weeks?" Her horror shifted to shock. "When can I go home?"

"Let's see how you do. We need to get you up and moving again and we'll run a few more tests. Then, we can talk about it. Okay?"

"Do I have a choice?"

Dr. Coleman gave her a smile that said she should know better than to even ask. Accepting her situation, Tess dropped her head back and let out a sigh. "Any chance I could get something to eat? I'm starving."

"I'll have something light sent up and I'll be back later to check on you."

Tess sat alone in her room, her thoughts swirling as she searched her mind for any recollection of the last few weeks. Coming up with nothing, she dragged her unbandaged right palm down her face and took a deep breath, flinching when she hit a tender spot on her cheek.

As a professional in the field of brain dysfunction, she knew she may never recover parts of her memory, yet that knowledge did nothing but frustrate her. Knowing only amplified her helplessness. Sitting still and stewing was not in her blood. Everyone in her family was a worker, a doer, a problem solver. She would have to apply her knowledge to herself, one step at a time, just like any of her clients.

She could do this. She could overcome. And she would.

CHAPTER NINETEEN

Portland - July 29, 2017

Thin shards of moonlight broke free of the curtains and bounced off the walls of Elena's bedroom. A gentle breeze swept through, jostling the dreamcatcher gift Mai had given her. Chloe stood up from the foot of the bed. The multicolored hairs on her back bristled for a split second before she calmed. Content there was no threat, she padded up to the pillows, curled up around Elena's head, and then descended into peaceful sleep.

The swirl of air made Elena snuggle further under her covers as she reached deep slumber. A smile warmed her lips in anticipation of her nightly date with the bluest eyes she had ever seen. She entered dreamland through a row of trees that led to an open field lined with the orange and yellow of fall. She expected to be welcomed into the strong arms she'd been craving. Instead, she arrived behind a young redheaded girl walking with her parents at what appeared to be some kind of fair.

Her disappointment was moved to awe when she was sucked into an omnipotent role, privy to the young girl's thoughts of both fear and desire. Their connection was deep, intimate, in a way Elena couldn't comprehend. A confusing onslaught of feelings swarmed her. Her heart overflowed with love, but her mind was devoid of hope. An internal battle waged without waver inside—such heaviness was carried by the young girl. It was exhausting and heartbreaking and Elena yearned to know more. What was the source of her pain and was there a way to help?

Elena followed close alongside, undetected by all, reading every thought, every experience, like they shared the same skin. Tempted to fight it, to run away and find the woman she longed for each time she closed her eyes, Elena took two steps back, but then stopped. Her desire to retreat was overruled by a powerful sense of purpose, as if there was something she was supposed to see that night instead of her blue-eyed dream girl.

Mai had always preached that dreams did not occur without reason, so there must have been some explanation for the sudden change. Accepting her fate, Elena relented, allowing the young girl to lead the way and herself to become one with her new guest—a guest the depths of her memory suddenly recognized as the fiancé in the old man's photo that day at the diner, Mary.

The mystery deepened.

Mary was on a desperate search. Someone extremely close to her heart, someone named Abbie, had a birthday in a few days. She was determined to find the perfect gift at the annual Cherokee Indian Fair.

Mary's fingers nervously massaged the two crisp one-dollar bills she held. She had been saving them for this special occasion. She glanced down at the face of President Washington and took a deep breath. Her focus fell on the black print signifying the year—1951. Abbie was turning sixteen, as would she in a few more weeks. The pressure to find the perfect gift mounted, because Abbie would no doubt go above and beyond for her.

The sky was blue, the air crisp, and fall had taken hold of the leaves. Mary walked with her parents along the venue's open field. There were several rows of sellers to wade through offering jewelry, clothes, knickknacks, and carvings. Hopefully, one of them would be unique and beautiful, like Abbie.

Mary left her parents behind and began a stroll through the vendors, making mental notes of all the items she was considering. She wouldn't choose lightly. Something would call to her, make her know without a doubt it should be "the gift," she was sure of it. And she was right.

Near the end of the second row of booths, she stopped at a table covered by intricate wood carvings of birds, fish, elk, nature scenes, and totems. Anything and everything she could imagine was cut into various types of wood with explicit detail. She lifted a flat piece of oak with a river scene that made her smile. When she glanced up in search of the owner, an old Cherokee man approached. His long white hair was tied back behind his shoulders, highlighting his round face and dark red skin. He eyed her carefully. Unlike the other Native American attendees adorned in buckskin or dance regalia, he was dressed simply in old blue jeans and a colorful button-down.

Instinctively, she folded inward and set the piece back as if she'd been reprimanded. His gaze was intense, almost scolding without words. For a moment she considered leaving, but the carving reminded her so much of their spot in the woods that it struck a chord. "How much please?" she asked timidly.

The old man stepped closer without addressing her question. He held his right hand out palm up. Unsure of his meaning, Mary pulled out her two dollars, unfolded them, and neatly placed them in his hand with eyes wide and brows high, silently asking if that was what he had wanted.

He shook his head and set the money down, before repeating his action. Mary was at a loss. Her inaction prompted him to reach for her hand. She recoiled in fear and the old man's dark brown eyes softened. He nodded and reached again. This time, Mary allowed him to take her hand and cup it between his two large, leathery ones. His eyes closed and his head dropped. Several seconds passed in silence as the old man remained still until finally, he raised his head and opened his eyes, meeting Mary's questioning brown one's head on.

"You seek gift for someone very special."

"Yes." Mary's eyes lit up. "How did you know?"

His gaze moved off to the left, as if he could see Elena standing beside her in the flesh, then returned to Mary. "Your soul shines. Your love is pure. And so is hers," he answered.

Mary looked away. Shame and embarrassment stained her neck and climbed higher, turning her face bright red.

"Love is love, young one. The spirit takes many journeys," he offered without judgement and gave her hand a squeeze. When Mary's eyes returned to him, they were rimmed with the threat of tears. "No journey is easy," he continued, "and it does not always find its mate."

He released her hand and walked to a box on the floor. He sifted through the contents, smiling wide when he found the intended mark. As he returned to her, he cradled a deerskin wrapped mystery item with tender care.

"What is it?" Mary inquired.

"A gift."

"A gift?"

"Yes." He set the object on the table and slowly unraveled the skin to reveal an eight-inch-tall great horned owl carved in cedar.

The detail was exquisite and Mary would swear the owl's eyes were real, despite their wooden origin. "Wow, it's beautiful. Yes, I would like to buy it. I only have the two dollars though. Is that enough?"

"No buy. Gift."

"That's very kind, but I couldn't. I-"

His large hand raised, cutting off her protest. "Two souls connected with such love is very rare. Only a gift given pure of heart is worthy. The owl is sacred in our culture. So is the cedar in which it is carved. They have achieved the height of purity and sacredness." The old man started to re-wrap the piece with delicate precision. "The journey will be very difficult for you both. This will help your spirits reunite and walk in light and love."

"Reunite?" Mary's mind reeled and she struggled to interpret his mystical words. Could he really see her future with Abbie? Doubtful, but either way, Mary couldn't imagine a life without her. They were best friends. No, they were more than that. What could ever drive them apart?

The many questions were silenced when the old man said, "May the Great Spirit walk with you." Once again, his eyes shifted left.

He held out a bag and Mary accepted it with an uneasy smile. "Thank you," she said and walked away. When she glanced back over her shoulder, he was nowhere to be found. She stopped in her tracks and spun around, looking left and right. A chill zipped up her spine.

"Mary."

The deep voice startled her. She jumped, nearly dropping her bag.

"We're ready to go," her father said as he strode past her in the direction of their car.

"Phillip, slow down." Her mother called out from behind. "He wants to get home in time for the football game." She hurried to catch up to Mary. "You know how he loves his Redskins," she stated casually, seeming not to notice the irony between the team mascot and the event they were attending. She stopped alongside and glanced at the bag. "Did you have fun, honey?"

"I did."

"What did you buy?"

"A birthday present for Abbie."

"Oh. That's nice." There was little effort to hide her disapproval. "Have you met that nice young boy that moved across the street yet? George, I believe his name is. Your father says he's very polite."

Mary rolled her eyes. George was about to become the latest in their set-up attempts. What was the rush? She was only fifteen. "No."

"We'll have to have them all over for dinner. That's the neighborly thing to do. Don't you think?" she asked with a smile.

There was no need to reply, but she responded in the affirmative anyway. They'd probably already set a date, but she would never know until the morning of. That's the way her parents tended to play these things, as if she would concoct some big plan to get out of it if she had prior notice. Honestly, she had considered trying. She could run to Abbie's arms under the guise of some fabled pre-planned event, but being the obedient daughter she was, she would buckle and agree time after time.

Mary climbed into the backseat of her family's 1946 Ford Woody Wagon and leaned back with a sigh. Tuning out the meaningless banter between her folks, she opened the bag and peeked inside. With one hand, she peeled back a section of the deerskin and ran her finger over the smooth cedar carved feathers of the owl. A tingle traversed her skin. The urge to hold the figure in her hands overwhelmed her and quick as a hummingbird, she had it unwrapped and clasped between her palms. Warmth enveloped her body and a smile was not to be contained. Eye to eye, she stared at the inanimate object that seemed to project more life than the flesh and blood beings blabbering on about a church sermon in the front seat.

Abbie was going to love it.

With a thundering in her chest, she re-wrapped the carving using as much care as the old man had, placed it back in the bag, and sat it securely in her lap. She didn't know what to think about spirits and journeys, but she loved Abigail with her whole heart and nothing would ever change that.

Elena's eyes fluttered open, her sleep disturbed by a tear gently caressing her cheek. Moonlight bathed the foot of her bed and silence embraced the world around her. Chloe lay above her head, her sleep undeterred by her mother's heavy heart.

Elena didn't know Mary or Abbie, but she had felt every bit of the weight Mary carried on her shoulders, heard every thought in her head, and understood every concern as if it were her own personal journey. She had moved throughout the dream scene, sometimes as a spectator, but mostly as if she had actually played the role of Mary, though the old Indian's words felt as if they had been meant for her as well. His presence had also brought with it an odd sense of comfort. The entire dream had been weird, yet so comfortable and natural that no true opinion could yet be formed on the experience.

She glanced up at the dreamcatcher. Just as she'd told Mai, her dreams had been evolving. The ones of her mysterious blue-eyed woman had turned more vivid, more determined, and now, a dream of a young woman in love with another and suffering the scorching pain of choosing love or family acceptance. The poor girl's heart teetered on a ledge between exploding with happiness and being ripped apart by the painful scorn of loved ones.

Every detail remained ingrained in Elena's mind to the point the dream mimicked her own personal reality, blurring the line between real life and fantasy. The leathery feel of the old Indian's hands as they wrapped around Mary's, as if he were holding her own. The smooth, solid feel of the owl's wooden form beneath her fingertips. Even the tingle that had zipped through Mary still buzzed high voltage across her skin.

If only she could have reached up and smacked Mary's parents. She casually wondered if she would have been able to make that happen.

Gently disengaging herself from Chloe, she rolled to her side and pushed up into a seated position. Elena rested her elbows on her knees and dropped her head into her hands. She really needed to talk to Grandma Mai about this, but it would have to wait until the sun came up. Considering the topic of conversation, maybe a little whiskey would be in order. Or, maybe a lot of whiskey.

Standing from the bed, she rubbed her hands back and forth over the shaved sides of her head to wake herself up. A quick glance back at Chloe left her envious. The calico had quickly claimed the warm spot she'd left behind and curled into a ball with a content grin.

Oh, to have a life like that, without a care in the world. But, she didn't. "Lucky cat," Elena muttered, then let out a hefty sigh. It was time to get back to reality.

She flipped on the light and as she passed her dresser on the way to the bathroom, she stopped and stared. Blue eyes stared back from a painting she had done a few weeks earlier. Her dream woman leaned against a bar top with arms crossed, a slight upward quirk of her lip, oozing confidence. Elena had painted her wearing a dark suit like the woman she had glimpsed at the Kansas City bar.

Elena couldn't peel her eyes away, as if magnets had been glued to her pupils that only held attraction for those mesmerizing sapphire blues. She shook her head and contemplated just how insane she might actually be. She really needed to get a grip.

"I wish I could stop thinking about you," she muttered, but didn't tear her eyes away. She'd almost swear she'd seen a shift in the painted woman's expression from confident to compassionate, as if she understood Elena's warring emotions all too well. *Insane, Elena. That's what you are.*

But even as she tried to convince herself of it, a sudden calm spread through her. Even on canvas, the woman held a power over her every thought, every feeling. She breathed in a deep breath, held it two seconds, then let it flow out. Her eyes drifted shut as she realized how much she had missed their visit last night.

"That's a lie. I'm happiest when I think of you," she said, her smile growing wider with every beat of her heart. After another long moment of locked gazes, a warm smile took up residence on her lips, evicting all apprehension. She hummed a soft tune as she walked away. Her thoughts still focused heavily on the woman in the painting and the many ways she affected her. Inspiration and longing. Those were the two that stood out beyond measure. At any given moment, Elena was in the midst of one emotion or the other.

More words came to her, flowing from her lips and released into the universe as she walked down the hall. They were words of truth, words pulled from her heart, words laced with the hope they'd one day allow her to spend more than just her nights with the woman in her dreams.

CHAPTER TWENTY

Atlanta - Same Night

The day had been long and draining. Tess was thankful to be out of the hospital, but she was bored and dealing with a severe case of cabin fever. Her days consisted of naps, home rehab, lounging on the couch, and twiddling her thumbs. Wasting time was a huge pet peeve of hers, unfortunately, she had no choice.

She was unable to do any work on her laptop. Even reading magazines, Tess could admit, was not pleasant. Her eyes and head protested the strain from her eyes, but that was what she loved. Reading was her relaxation. Never mind if the topics were hopeless case studies, psychotic episodes, or heartbreaking effects of terrible diseases. Neuropsychology was her passion and she would devour every new piece of information she could scrounge.

Instead, she was laying around in low light, trying as hard as possible to do as little as possible while her brain healed. Turning in at nine o'clock in the middle of summer and pulling the blackout curtains closed seemed sad, as if the early bird special would be her next stop. "You know how these things work, Tess,"

Dr. Coleman had said. "It'll take time. The brain has its own schedule and no one can predict how long, or what path you'll have to navigate during recovery."

"I know, I know," she grumbled to herself and settled deeper into her pillow. Knowing and doing were two very different things and patience had never been one of Tess's strengths when it came to her own affairs. She had always done what she wanted, when she wanted. But she was trying.

Practicing her deep breathing exercises, she closed her eyes, settled her mind, and drifted off.

∞ ∞ ∞

"I wish I could stop thinking about you."

Tess rocketed straight up in bed. A shiver raced up her spine. "Who's in here?" she asked. Her sleep filled eyes strained through the darkness, cringing when they reached the glaring green neon light of her clock that read 4:15 a.m. The eerie silence that followed had her skin crawling like ten thousand ants scurrying across her flesh. Every inner warning known to man jumped to attention.

"That's a lie. I'm happiest when I think of you."

"Me? Who are you? Why are you in my room?" Without a face to identify, all she had was a voice. A woman's voice. Who would do such a thing?

She immediately thought of a former client, Sky, who had not been shy about her affections. Had she survived the truck only to be murdered by her psychotic stalker?

In a slow, non-threatening movement, Tess reached over and turned on the light. Her eyes slammed shut at the unwelcomed invasion of her senses. Just the flash had been enough to make her head pound again. "Owww, dammit!"

"Some people conjure visions of beaches or mountains..."

"Shut up. Go away." One eye cracked open to examine the room. Her fear went unconfirmed, but it was much worse than imagined. The room was empty.

"But I have you. I don't know why, but you bring me peace."

"I'd like some peace myself." *This is bad. So very bad.* Tess turned the light off and held her head. Her upper body rocked back and forth, an instinctual attempt to soothe herself, until a knock on the door made her groan.

"Tess? You okay?" Evan asked through the white wooden door.

"Right as rain."

"That's some bullshit, but I like your enthusiasm."

She chuckled, then grabbed her head again as a sharp stab arced over her left ear. Gritting her teeth, she did her best to snuff out a scream of pain. She wasn't in the mood to see anyone—especially not Evan.

"Seriously though?"

"I'm fine. Just a nightmare." *Or worse. A voice in my head is definitely worse.*

Silence.

"Really, Evan. I'm okay." *I hope.* "Thanks for checking on me."

"Always. Okay then, let me know if you need anything."

"I will. Goodnight, Evan."

"Goodnight, Tess."

As Evan's steps faded, Tess noted no other voices and she reveled in the silence. A relieved sigh filled the room, though she was anything but. The pounding of her heart throbbed in her head and goosebumps still stood at attention across her skin.

She had treated and reviewed hundreds of cases over the years, not to mention the countless research papers and seminars about this very topic, but reality had blown through the door and gotten right up in her face in some sick attempt to show her how little she really knew.

The revelation was a Holly Holm-sized kick to the stomach, and worse yet, Tess silently resigned, studying others had done little to prepare her for her own affliction.

∞ ∞ ∞

Early afternoon brought with it a light tap on her bedroom door, pulling Tess from the sleep it had taken her hours to find after last night's experience. "Hmph?" she grunted, barely awake.

"It's me. Just checking on you. You're usually up early."

An eye peered out through a crack to see the clock. She was surprised to see 1:17 p.m. The rest had been solid and it was the best she'd felt since she had awoken from her coma, physically anyway. Mentally, she was a wreck, as if her physical body and mind had switched places.

Her arms stretched overhead and she rolled onto her back. "Come on in, Evan."

Her door slowly creaked open. Blond hair led his entrance as he craned his neck inside. He looked her over suspiciously, eyes narrowing at her amused grin.

"Really. Come in. I'm fine. Feeling really good actually, though the um..." she paused. Not wanting to discuss what had really happened, she kept to her original excuse. "Nightmare had kept me up a while."

"I could have helped," he said as he approached.

"You've done so much and I appreciate all of it, but there are some things I need to work through on my own."

He sat on the edge of her bed. "I know. It's hard to watch though."

Tess covered his hand with hers and gave it a squeeze. She looked into a pair of blue eyes that matched her own. "I understand. I'm sure I'd be going crazy if our roles were reversed." *Great choice of words. I may be going crazy anyway.* She swallowed hard and looked away. "Enough sadness. When's the next date with your new girl?"

He beamed at the mention of the woman. "Tomorrow night, actually. Dinner and the new sci-fi movie. Can you believe she loves the old ones from the sixties too?"

"Wow. A woman that shares your passion for ancient science fiction? She must be a winner."

A laugh snuck out and he said, "Time will tell, but I really like her. We just kind of click, ya know?"

"Mhm," was her reply, but she didn't. Not really. In theory, yes. She'd studied the concept and had done an internship with a relationship counselor in college, but personally, not even close.

As if struck by a thought, Evan paused. His smile dropped to a frown and he chewed the corner of his lip. "Sorry," he said, inexplicably apologizing.

Confused, Tess asked, "For what?"

"I know you and Amy broke up."

If he only knew it had actually been a relief. "Thanks. It's okay. Not everyone is meant to be. I'm still happy for you. I hope to meet her soon."

"Thanks. And you will definitely meet her soon if things keep going well." Evan paused once more, growing uncomfortable yet again. "Umm...speaking of Amy, she called to see how you were doing."

He must have thought it would upset her, but quite the opposite. Even after Tess had broken her heart, Amy was still concerned about her. She was a sweetheart and deserved better than what she could give. "That was nice of her. I'll uh...I'll give her a call soon."

"Good. That would be good." An uncomfortable silence remained for long seconds before he spoke again. "I really liked her. She was good for you. I thought you two would last. Can I ask what happened? I mean, if you don't mind."

Tess considered his statement. Amy had been good for her in many ways, but not in that one, all-important, but seemingly unattainable way. "Amy is an amazing woman and we had fun, but unlike you two, we didn't click. At least, not in the right ways, or enough ways...I don't...I can't explain it, but-"

"She's just not the one," he finished for her, a statement rather than a question.

"Right."

"There's someone out there for you."

"I'm fine with the life I have, Evan. Not everyone needs that 'other half' to be fulfilled." That came out more harshly than intended, so she quickly added, "Not that there's anything wrong with that. Love, a partner...those are important. The human need to socialize and mate are basic needs for most people. Could be I'm more highly evolved," she teased and rolled to her side, then pushed herself up into a seated position beside him.

He laughed. "Then I hope your evolution includes the ability to perform asexual reproduction so the human race doesn't die out."

They shared a laugh. "Noted. I'll work on that while I'm busy in my hermitage."

"Good." He stood from the bed and then watched as she got to her feet, still wary of her dizzy spells.

Today, however, she was swift and steady, unlike the days previously when her head would spin and her body would wobble. A smile pulled at both of their lips in celebration of her victory.

"I've got lunch made if you're hungry. Oh, and Natalie called. She'd love to come see you, if you're up to it."

"I'm starving. I'll be down in ten. And thank you, I'd love to see her. I'll give her a call back."

With a parting nod, Evan left Tess alone to freshen up. The sunshine shooting through the gaps in the curtain wasn't as painful as yesterday. Another little victory. She grabbed a pencil and slipped it into her cast, scratching the irritated skin with a frustrated groan. When enough of the itch had been relieved, she pulled off her shirt on the way to the bathroom. Her reflection in the mirror made her pause.

The woman staring back looked much the same as before. Blue eyes. Sharp jawline. Slim nose. Mole above her left brow. Only now, a scar marred the skin above her left brow and the left side of her chin. The whitened remains of road rash speckled her right shoulder. Then, of course, there was the cast.

The souvenirs were by no means hideous, but still signs that she had changed and they meant a lifetime of reminders of a day she would rather forget. The fleshy exterior of her body had been altered and so had the delicate tissue in her head, forever damaged to some unknown degree.

The question she wanted answered would only come in time. Would the voice be a side effect of healing on a passing visit or a permanent resident in her mind?

Either way, she needed to cope with her situation and hope her own personal experience turned out better than Rod's so she could help others later.

CHAPTER TWENTY-ONE

Portland - August 7, 2017

Their fingers threaded delicately together like silk on the finest dress. For the second time, Elena found herself shadowing Mary in her dream. This time, however, she was more than happy to play along.

Mary smiled at Abbie, whose sapphire-blue eyes illuminated her world with all the love they held for her—eyes remarkably similar to those belonging to the woman who held Elena's heart. Elena had understood why there was no place Mary would rather be than by Abbie's side walking hand in hand along a river in the forest.

A part of her was jealous, wishing she had been the one doing this very thing with a very different woman. Her heart thumped a little faster, causing a passing bout of dizziness that affected both she and Mary. *Interesting.*

"You all right?" Abbie asked.

Elena snapped to, but handed the reins to Mary. She didn't want to derail however this was supposed to playout by inserting her own fantasy. It was Mary's world, after all. Elena was merely a passenger in search of some hidden meaning. So, she sat back and watched. And *felt.*

"Yes. I'm wonderful. I'm with you." Mary's words soothed Abbie's concern and she followed it with a smile that emanated the truth from the very depths of her soul. The girl standing in front of her never ceased to make her heart skip and jump, her stomach to flip and flop, and her skin to tingle and flush bright red. Abigail Carter had stolen her heart in the fourth grade when she'd beaten up Henry Benson for shoving her in the mud. Ever since then, Mary had lived to embrace every next occurrence of blissful dizziness and feverish joy.

Abbie squeezed her hand, then brought it to her lips for a kiss. There it was again, one of those little moments that electrified her body and set her blood pumping so hard she could hear it whooshing in her ears. Abigail Carter may have been all woman, but she was more of a gentleman than any of the boys she had ever met.

"The spot is just up ahead. Shall we?"

Giving Abbie an agreeable nod, she was led to a hidden gem. A small cove formed of rocks with a path of stones that trailed halfway out into the river. They were surrounded by tall sugar maples that provided the perfect amount of privacy while enveloping them with the relaxing sound of water carving its way over nature's obstacles. Together they spread out the blanket and opened the picnic basket.

"It's perfect, Abbie. How did you find this place?"

"I snuck out one night after Momma and Kenny made me mad."

"You were out here alone? At night? Abigail Carter!" Mary scolded.

"It's fine. I'm fine. I took my knife with me. Besides, it gave us this." Abbie threw her arms out, spreading them as wide as the smile on her face as she spun in a circle.

"What will I ever do with you?"

"Just love me."

"I do. I will. Always." Mary caressed Abbie's cheek softly, then cupped it with her hand. She was drawn in, as always, to soft lips and inviting arms that made her forget the rest of the world that shunned them. She wanted it to last forever, for Abbie's strength to carry them both. For now, however, none of that mattered, because they were here. Together.

A low moan emanated from Abbie when Mary's hand slipped under her shirt. Quivering lips sought purchase once again and Mary allowed them to indulge, their tongues dancing, chests heaving, breaths short in the most addicting way.

"I love you," Mary whispered between kisses.

"And I love you," was returned as their movement slowed and their eyes met.

"Touch me." The honesty of the moment weighed heavy in the air. Mary considered herself a good girl. She went to church and obeyed her parents, mostly, but she was seventeen now and had loved Abbie for the last eight years. Some days she could cry from the amount of want coursing through her body. Fantasies were great and all, but this was a reality she was done denying herself. "Please."

Abbie's breath hitched. "Are you sure? We don't ha-"

"I dream of us...together...like that. Of how soft your strong hands would be in places no one else has touched and how your skin would feel against mine as we lay together."

A light shimmer flashed in Abbie's eyes. "Me too," she admitted, her voice full of tenderness and adoration.

A slow smile spread up her cheeks to light her eyes and Mary stepped back one pace. Her finger tips slowly slipped the straps of her yellow flowered dress from her shoulders, grinning wider at the entranced look upon Abbie's face. It was a powerful feeling to hold someone captive in such a way and Mary was thoroughly enjoying her newfound command.

The dress pooled around her feet, leaving her in a white slip that barely hid her white cotton underwear and pert breasts. Abbie had yet to move, so Mary closed the gap and let her nimble fingers deftly undo the buttons of her lover's blue shirt. It was her favorite, as it matched the color of Abbie's eyes.

As Mary pushed the fabric off a set of toned shoulders and onto the floor, she also learned that she loved Abigail in no shirt at all. Her fingers itched to touch every centimeter of exposed flesh and her body begged to receive the same attention in return.

She couldn't say which desire screamed louder, but she was determined to quiet them both.

Mary slowly directed them to the ground, lying side by side on the soft cotton blanket. Her fingers blazed a trail up Abbie's arm, across her collar bone, and through the valley between a pair of creamy white breasts, leaving a path of goosebumps in their wake. She was spellbound and the woman she loved was at her mercy, frozen in time with lips parted, desperately wanting more as she arched into her touch. It was the most beautiful thing Mary had ever seen.

Or so she had thought.

That moment came later, as Abigail Carter unraveled before her eyes, moving in time with her fingers and moaning her name into the depths of the forest. She would never love anyone more.

Elena's eyes opened to a haze of unshed tears. Another dream so amazingly vivid and real had left her with feelings—deep, overwhelming feelings—flowing in and out of every cell in her body. She'd never experienced such love, but she wanted to more than anything. Had she become some sad cliché?

"Get a grip, Elena. It was just a dream," she admonished herself. The words left a bitter taste in her mouth and a lingering damper on her heart. There was more to them and she needed to figure it out. She did learn one thing—Abbie was the reason for Mary's forced smile in that old photo.

She wiped her eyes with the back of her hand and rolled onto her side. The sun was just breaking the horizon and a new day had arrived. With the exception of her father's death, it was only the second time since she was a young girl that she hadn't dreamt of the woman.

Those blue eyes of Abbie's though...so eerily familiar, shining with the same warmth and love...it was as if she had actually spent the night with her dark-haired beauty. Well, almost. She didn't usually have a third-wheel named Mary in her fantasies.

The change of pace left an empty place in her heart, just as it had the first time, but her body remained warm from the love she'd felt between the two young girls. Was the change of pace good? Did it mean she would slowly dream less and less of her blue-eyed beauty?

The thought pierced sharp like a knife through her chest. Crazy or not, that was not what she wanted. Rubbing the skin above her pounding heart to ease the remaining ache, she tried putting a positive spin on the new events. *Perhaps today is the day I finally find Her.*

CHAPTER TWENTY-TWO

Portland - August 9, 2017

Mai greeted Elena with her usual warm hug and contagious smile. The moment Elena was released, Mai picked up two cups of tea, handed one to Elena, and then walked to the living room. "I've been doing some research since your last visit, but after your phone call, I had an idea," she said as she set the tea down. She lowered herself into her favorite old chair. "And the changes in your dreams do fit my theory."

Elena smiled and sat across from her. Mai loved these kinds of mysteries. There was no doubt she had scoured every resource available. "And what is your theory?"

"Some tribes believe we have two souls, one in the waking world and one at night. The night soul wanders to far lands when we dream, even across the physical plane where those we have lost await our arrival. In that, it is reasonable to assume that your night soul could also interact with other souls. Perhaps ones you knew in past lives."

"I respect our culture, but this all sounds so…"

"Ridiculous?"

"Well...yeah. Kinda. Doesn't it?"

Mai laughed. "It does to many, but I have witnessed my share of unexplainable things in my life. I don't pretend to understand them, but I trust and believe that there are plenty of things that defy our comprehension or explanation. The universe holds so many mysteries, both beautiful and frightening." Mai paused and drummed her fingers on the arm of the chair. "Of course, you could always choose to ignore the dreams and keep living your life."

"I'm not sure I'm living much of a life," Elena admitted.

Mai smiled an all-knowing smile that required no words of acknowledgment and waited patiently as Elena pondered her choices.

Could pursuing Mai's theory be worse than her current situation? She was almost afraid to find out, but she couldn't continue her current course without truly going insane. "Okay, ignoring it is not an option. So, what's choice number two?" Elena asked timidly.

"You could let me show you the deep meditation exercise that has been passed down in our family for generations. It has helped me find my way many times."

"Ugh." A heavy breath flowed through her lips as Elena rolled her neck. She had never been a fan of meditation or visualization. It was too slow and felt forced. She preferred free flowing methods, such as her artwork, to center herself and release stress. However, other than an overabundance of paintings of the same woman, she acknowledged that her current methods were failing.

Her body folded inward in submission and like a stubborn child finally conceding to her parental, she said, "I would love it if you'd show me."

A satisfied smile pulled at the corners of Mai's mouth. She brought her hands together, all ten finger tips touching, as if contemplating some grand plan. "Very well then. Let's get started."

∞ ∞ ∞

Two hours, three reprimands for losing focus, and far too many old, brown books later, Elena was experiencing information overload. She needed to get out and process. The theory alone was mind boggling, but there was also a ton of spiritual lore, Native American and then some. On top of that, there was the ritual itself, although that wasn't too complicated. The problem was, she had to believe and that was something she was struggling with at the moment. It was all too far-fetched.

Why was this happening to her? What made her so special?

"One last thing," Grandma Mai said as Elena tried to make her escape.

She turned with an exhausted groan and grumbled, "What?"

Mai ignored her irritation and waved her back. She retrieved a hand-carved wooden talisman from a box and placed it in Elena's hands with tender care. "Here. This is your connection to the spirit world. The meditation is wonderful for finding your way in life, but to cross the plane and communicate with another soul, you will need a spirit guide. Our family's guide is the bear."

"What do I do with it?"

"Hold it or place it in front of you. The bear may appear in its natural form, as a human, or you may feel a gentle nudge toward what you seek."

Elena's fingers curled around the carved wood, tracing the outlines of the animals as if memorizing it for future reference. The feel of the wood jogged memories of the carved owl in her dream. Eerie, yet again, oh so right.

She nodded, though her belief remained weak. Spirits and rituals, while they had been a part of her upbringing, held little weight. Her mother would tell unbelievable tales of her time with the Chinook shaman and Grandma Mai, but Elena had never witnessed any proof herself.

As free spirited and artistic as she was, she often took after her scientist father and tended to err on the side of tangibles and logic. Though admittedly, the diner episode with the old man had been quite the mystical event. Then, of course, there were the dreams. Those alone should be proof enough that there was so much more to the universe.

So, why was it so hard for her to give in and believe? Maybe because it felt as if next they'd be discussing genies and wizards.

"I know that look, Elena, but you have to believe. Open yourself to the energy of the universe around you. It's not held by the boundaries you can see. It is never ending and all-encompassing. Perhaps you're not ready now, but when you are, you'll have the tools you need."

CHAPTER TWENTY-THREE

Portland - August 12, 2017

Thin rays of morning sun peeked through the living room blinds and caressed Elena's back. Ignoring their soothing warmth, she held the wooden talisman tight to her chest and sat Indian style on a hand-woven Chinook rug. She stared down at its delicate crisscrossing fibers. The repeating pattern of black and red diamonds with horizontal stripes turned hypnotic, bringing her much needed calm.

In the three nights since she'd last seen Mai, the dreams had intensified. Last night's had been the most realistic yet and her heart literally ached when she had awoken to her reality—alone.

I can't go on like this.

Her eyelids drifted closed and, as instructed, she focused on the dark-haired woman in her dreams with searing blue eyes that warmed her soul and a low-timbered voice that resonated deep within her being. Though all doors and windows were sealed, a warm breeze touched her skin, just like the one that had caressed her last night in the arms of her lover as they kissed passionately in the forest on a summer day. It would be so easy to relive that memory over and over, but that was no longer enough. Her poor heart either needed more or she needed closure. Come what may, it was time to reach out.

Maintaining her focus, Elena took a deep cleansing breath and looked her blue-eyed dream woman in the eye. "Hi. I don't know what I'm doing really, but at this point, I'll try anything."

This is so weird. As the brief moment of doubt crept in, her door to the other world began to close, obscuring her lover from sight. Elena's heart clenched and she quickly steeled herself. Her focus returned with unprecedented determination, blowing the door wide open.

I can do this. I will do this.

She stepped through the doorway and into a realm of the whitest white she had ever seen. Elena was forced to shield her eyes until a pair of sympathetic blazing blues came into view. They dripped with as much hope as sadness, as if the heartache could be felt both ways. Was it even possible? There was only one way to find out.

"I don't know who or where you are, or why you have such a hold on my heart, but I feel you. Every night I see you and it's like we live another life together. And every morning, I wake feeling empty." Elena paused for a deep breath, feeling the honesty in her words. If she was going to throw it out into the universe, she was going all in. What was there to lose?

"No one I've ever met could live up to you and that's ridiculous because...well...you're not even real. Or, I guess you are...somewhere...but not here. Point is, I'd like you to be...real...here with me."

Elena's honest words received a tear in response from her silent companion. Though she hadn't really expected a conversation, she had hoped for one. With no further acknowledgement or effort from the other woman, she saw no reason to continue. Seemed she wouldn't be getting any of the answers she had so desperately sought, but perhaps planting a seed of suggestion would prove whether or not any of this had ever been real. That had to be something. Right?

"Anyway," Elena began, "I'm sure I will see you tonight." She stepped closer, extending her hand, but the woman was always out of reach. Elena sighed and dropped her head. "If you are real somewhere, and you can hear me, can you find a way to let me know? I really need to know. Okay?"

The woman only stared, confusion peppering the contours of her face as if processing the request, but she never responded. Her bright blue eyes dimmed and she turned to leave. A pulsing white light in the distance seemed to call to her, but she stopped and glanced over her shoulder to meet Elena's solemn gaze once more.

For a moment, it appeared as if she were attempting to struggle against an invisible force in an effort to return to Elena, to reach out and accept the offered hand. But it was not to be. Whatever power had a hold of her was too much to overcome.

Confusion turned to sadness as she was pulled farther and farther away. The light grew dim, as did Elena's hope that tonight's dreams would have a new ending.

∞ ∞ ∞

Atlanta - Same Day

A flash of pain arced across Tess's right temple. Her eyes pressed shut tight and her teeth ground as she cringed, hoping it would pass quickly. Thankfully, episodes had grown less frequent, as had the headaches, but she was still a long way from healed.

"You all right, Tess?"

"Yeah. Just a headache coming on." She pushed her recliner shut and leaned forward to rest her head in her hands.

"Have you still been getting them often? Do we need another scan?"

"No. No. No more scans. It's not that bad and they are much less frequent." She peeked through one half-lidded lens, then inwardly groaned at his intense inspection.

Evan had scooted to the edge of the cushy black leather sofa, elbows on knees leaning toward her. His brow flexed with concern, crushing the relaxed features that had been present mere seconds ago when he'd been reading from his favorite old science fiction novel, "Fahrenheit 451," for the eight hundredth time.

Maybe it was time to go back to her house. The constant babysitting was frustrating. "Probably stress. You know how I hate sitting around. I'm fine."

"I know, but please do what they say. You…you were bad off, Tess. I really thought I'd lost you. I'm not ready for that. Not after mom and dad."

The sadness in Evan's eyes and the weight of his admission hit her hard. Staying here wasn't really all that bad. She was lucky to have someone who cared so deeply for her wellbeing. So many of her clients had no one. Worse yet, their loved ones had abandoned them. If it made him feel better, then she could deal a while longer. "I know. I will. I just…ugh. I want to do research on my tablet."

"You know you can't." He shook his head and relaxed, sinking back into the cushions. "No screens until they clear you. Besides, it bothers you to read anyway."

"But at least I'd feel productive." She rubbed at her temples in a feeble attempt to reduce the pain.

"I understand that, but think of it as a vacation. You haven't had one in…" he searched his memory banks with a tilt of his head, "at least six years, that I know of. Not since the week-long cruise with that girl. What was her name?"

Her other eye popped open as she shot him a glare. "That was a disaster. Never again." The memory alone was enough to bring on a massive migraine. Why she had ever agreed was still a mystery. The entire trip consisted of arguments that she was flirting with every woman on board. Okay, so she had flirted with a couple of them, but that was near the end of the trip when she had gotten fed up with Taylor's accusations.

"What? Cruises? I love them," he emphatically professed.

Tess rolled her eyes. "No, not cruises in general. Going on a cruise with a date. Cruises are much better suited for the single life."

Evan laughed and picked up his book, releasing Tess from the weight of his heavy scrutiny. The ache in her head was slowly dissipating, relaxing her contracted muscles. She breathed deep in relief. When she eased back into her recliner, an uncomfortable tug at the back of her mind sent her into an upright position. She craned her neck over her shoulder expecting to find someone else in the room. The hairs on the back of her neck sprang to life and a shiver raced down her spine. Tess glanced at her brother who had shifted his attention back to his novel without any ounce of alarm.

"I don't know what I'm doing really, but at this point, I'll try anything."

She whipped her head around, but still no one. "Is anyone else here?"

Evan raised his eyes from his book, a brow arched in question. "Just you and me, like always. Why?"

"I thought I heard a voice."

"I didn't hear anything."

Tess looked around again, this time standing and walking the room, ignoring the way Evan studied her every move. She came to a stop in front of the window, but the afternoon sun was too much for her senses and quickly chased her away. The feeling snuck up on her again, resulting in the same hair-raising chills.

"I don't know who or where you are, or why you have such a hold on my heart, but I feel you. Every night I see you and it's like we live another life together. And every morning, I wake feeling empty."

Tess took a breath and called upon her skills of analysis to assess the situation. Her physical response seemed to be linked to the return of the woman's voice and, as she suspected, she was the only one who could hear *Her*. This time, however, as alarming as the feeling was and as frightening as it was to have a stranger's voice in her head, fear kept at bay.

In fact, interestingly enough, quite the opposite took hold. The voice offered a comfort she had never experienced. So familiar, yet unrecognizable. Was it the voice of someone she had known? Some subconscious recall due to her trauma?

There weren't any other explanations, at least not ones that would keep her from losing her license and being committed. Tess was a professional and knew the audible hallucination had to be a side effect of her brain injury, but this...it felt so very intimate, like she could feel another presence nearby.

The memory of that night in her room came roaring back. It had been a week, so Tess had chalked it up to some weird aberration due to fatigue or medications. But here it was again.

She shifted uncomfortably and strained to listen for any further words, hoping more would come. Was it strange to find herself intrigued rather than fearful or concerned, as she most certainly should be? Look what happened to Rod. Had his condition progressed this very same way?

"No one I've ever met can live up to you and that's ridiculous, because...well, you're not even real. Or, I guess you are...somewhere...but not here. Point is, I'd like you to be...real...here with me."

The words spoke to Tess's heart. She couldn't pinpoint why, but they had moved her soul on a deep level to the point she believed she'd do anything to grant the woman's wish.

"Anyway, I'm sure I will see you tonight. If you are real somewhere, and you can hear me, find a way to let me know. I really need to know. Okay?"

"Tonight?" Her question passed under her breath and fled into the great beyond as her headache eased.

"What's tonight?" Evan inquired, his eyes still concentrated on her.

"Huh?" she asked, not realizing she'd spoken aloud. "Nothing." She shook her head. "I'm feeling better now."

"Good," he replied, though the look on his face said he was clearly not convinced. "I'll be making dinner soon. You should get some rest. And make sure you're drinking plenty of water."

"Yes, doctor." She smiled and accepted the offered glass, the remainder of his own water. "It's not whiskey, but it'll do."

"Whiskey, huh?" He laughed.

"Well, almost dying certainly isn't a pinot moment."

"Very true. We'll be sure to toast when you're fully cleared. In the meantime, what would you like to do tonight?"

She shrugged. There weren't many options for her. Scrabble was getting old and she was in no mood for company, but mostly, she couldn't stop wondering about the voice. Was something else in store tonight? Was that the voice of the Grim Reaper? Would this be her last day? If so, she would be sure to tell Evan she loved him before sleep.

"Whatever you like, Evan. Thank you for everything. You know I love you, right?"

He smiled up at her and said, "I do and I love you too, Tess. Sleep well."

As Tess made her way to her room, the words spoken by *Her* replayed on a loop. They still made her heart clench and as passionately as she felt about hearing that sweet voice again tonight, the eerie feeling that this may be a nap she never wakes from swirled in her belly. She paused and took one last look at Evan relaxing in the other room. At least she was at peace with the one person she loved.

∞ ∞ ∞

Last night, Tess's sleep had been bombarded by a plethora of incomprehensible scenes, none of which had been the eventful night she had hoped for. There was no communication with the voice that had been plaguing her. Instead, she was struck with the images of two young girls, one blonde, one redhead, holding hands in a forest. Next, they were riding in a car. Then, she was approached by the curvy figure of a dark-haired woman with a hand outstretched toward her. With the exception of her deep brown eyes, her face had been blurred. No matter how hard Tess had tried to close the distance, the woman had remained just out of reach. Tess had even attempted to ask questions, but her words fell on deaf ears. Finally, she woke up.

She was soaked to the bone and more exhausted than a late night of dancing with Natalie. A feeling of frustration and longing lingered and had left her irritable all morning. On the plus side, she did wake up, so she had that going for her.

As mid-afternoon arrived, a mild headache began a steady thump behind Tess's eyes. She'd had very few lately and when they did strike, they were usually associated with the voice.

Her mouth pulled tight in annoyance. She had finally been given the go ahead to do some light reading and she was not in the mood to be interrupted. Her eyes fell back to the black text on glossy white paper, determined to finish the article. A light breeze rustled the edge of her page.

"Those eyes..."

Tess's attention piqued when the familiar silvery voice made an abrupt return. It most certainly wasn't the voice of Evan's old college friend who had left an hour ago. Thank goodness, because her voice was nasally and high pitched and everything that grated Tess's nerves, now more than ever. But this voice had always been pleasing to the ear, the kind that left you wanting more, and like childhood story time, Tess was itching to listen.

The psychology journal fell into her lap and she threw a glance at her brother, who was fully engrossed in his laptop. Content she wouldn't be disturbed, she relaxed back and awaited whatever came next.

"I paint them, draw them, dream of them. Blue as the summer sky reflected in a crystal-clear mountain lake. I happily dive in, swim in them, bathe myself in the love they shine only for me. I had never worried about losing myself in them night after night, drawing after drawing, but each visit I swim farther from shore, and now I fear I may lack the strength to ever return."

Unlike the first two experiences, Tess took the time to admire the velvety, passion-filled sound as she once again analyzed the situation. Weird that *She* wasn't talking to her, like most cases Tess had studied. Rather, they were random musings, like Rod had reported. But these couldn't possibly be from the depths of her own mind. Or, could they? She had never considered herself a wordsmith or a woman of such romantic depth and she certainly lacked all artistic talent.

"I could drown in them, sink into the depths of blue. It would be a wonderful way to go, but something inside tells me to keep swimming, that I will one day reach the other side and you'll be waiting for me."

If the voice was a manifestation of her own doing, she much preferred the sound of it to her own. Plus, she'd love to tap into that poetic side. She'd get better at breakups. Tess laughed to herself, but was quickly broken from her thoughts by the start of another verse.

"No longer just a dream, you'll pull me into your very real and strong arms, rescue me, yet plunge me deeper still as I finally witness the reality of their true color in the flesh. Air will escape me, as will words, but you will save me again. Your lips pressed to mine, breathing life into me, a life I had always wished for, but never thought I could have. A life with you. Could it be true?

"I pray it is. For what else is there to wish for if everything I've ever wished for could only ever live in my work and my dreams? So now I prepare to close my eyes, taking one last deep breath before sleep arrives, hoping it carries me to the other side. Then, when morning comes, I awake to find that light and love has followed me home and at last, I would have you, whoever you are."

Tears slipped free and Tess rushed to wipe them away. The words, while shocking and scary to hear in her own head, were so touching, so poignant, that her heart clenched, reaching a place deep inside that made her want to be the savior.

But wait. A moment of rational thought begged an important question. Wouldn't hearing voices mean she needed her own savior?

Rod entered her mind again and fear tiptoed in as stealthy as a cat on the hunt. If she ever needed to find a cure for whatever was plaguing her, it would be now.

CHAPTER TWENTY-FOUR

Portland - August 17, 2017

With each stroke of the brush, Marlie stood mesmerized by the confidence Elena exuded in her execution. The picture flowed out of her and poured onto the canvas as if she had painted the very same picture a million times over. As Elena worked diligently, her image taking form, Marlie directed her attention to the row of finished work along the warehouse wall.

One canvas after the next she studied them, taking her time to admire the detailed strokes and fine lines. But more than that, Marlie admired the subject. The woman with long, flowing dark hair was featured in each of the twelve paintings, some as a portrait, and others more abstract. There she was, front and center, from a profile pose to a partial nude in every medium Elena used; black and white, color, oils, pencils, chalk, and even stippling. The eyes, a brilliant blue, were a mesmerizing combination of bold and warm as they focused on her, though they held a touch of sadness and longing that made her want to weep.

One piece stood out above all else, stirring Marlie's soul as the sea would a sailor, daring her to ignore its call. The dark-haired woman stood beside a river under a canvas of maple trees in simple blue jeans and a white T-shirt. Her bare feet were buried in lush green grass. The bright colors of autumn burst from the painting in such full detail that Marlie swore she was standing right in the middle of it breathing in the crisp air.

As Marlie's eyes carried her toward the back of the scene, the color faded slowly, as did the focus, until there was nothing but bright light. Not yellow or orange like the sun, but a white light born of various shades to demonstrate rays stretching into the forest. The shift was almost painful, seeing the color stripped away.

The woman, who was as equally defined in meticulous detail, wore an expression of love and hope, her hand outstretched toward the front edge, begging for it to be accepted. Blue eyes burned intensely, but were laced with a sadness that made Marlie want to grant her request. But the offer was not for her. From the bottom right corner, another's fingers, a woman's, reached inward, but did not touch. A hopeful union. A wish unfulfilled. A love denied. So many feelings on one canvas.

Everything about it seemed to speak of the feelings Elena had described from her dreams. So close, but so infinitely far away. An ache pierced Marlie's chest and she felt for her friend. She choked back the lump in her throat. She hadn't truly understood the depth of their conversations until now. "Not haunting you, huh?"

"Like I said, haunting would imply something bad." Elena set her brush down and walked to Marlie's side. She stared at the painting. Her head tipped left in examination, then she said, "Nothing about this feels bad or scary."

"She's beautiful."

"She is." Elena smiled, one that beamed from the inside out without control. "She drives me crazy every bit as much as she fuels my imagination."

Marlie couldn't miss Elena's sudden glow of happiness. How she wished it would shine for someone real. "Looking at these drawings, I would have to agree. This work is very inspired. Some of your best."

"Thank you. The gallery in Seattle called. They want to do a show."

"That's great, Elena." Marlie wrapped her into a tight, congratulatory hug.

"Yeah. Thank you." Elena hugged her back, but then pulled away. Her weight shifted, giving away her discomfort. "I was umm...thinking," her eyes roamed everywhere except Marlie, "it might be time for a change."

A brief moment of silence fell before Marlie hesitantly asked, "What do you mean?"

"Possibly a move, or at least a long road trip after I set it up." Elena ducked her head, but glanced up through her lashes as she awaited a response.

A gasp fell out as Marlie's brows rose. "You're leaving me?"

"Never." Elena smiled with sincerity and placed her hand on Marlie's arm. "But I have to find me, you know? I don't feel like I belong here. I may not feel any different anywhere else, but I have to get out of here and find out."

"I understand." Marlie moved to pull her into another hug, this one lingering as if it was the last time they would ever see one another. Her heart hurt at the thought of Elena leaving, but recognized her need to search out some semblance of sanity. Unfortunately, her efforts here had been fruitless. "I'll miss you like crazy, but you know I support you. Wherever you end up, I hope you find what you need. And I'll always be here for you."

"Thanks, Marlie." Elena returned the embrace with just as much emotion.

"So, you haven't made any progress with, you know…?" Marlie nudged her head toward the woman in the painting.

The look on Elena's face said it all. They freed one another from their embrace and stared at the canvas. "Not really." Elena took a deep breath and looked away as she continued, "I've been doing the meditation as Grandma explained and there was a time or two that my dreams were different, but ultimately, I'm still a crazy lady," she finished with a sad laugh.

"You're not crazy. Maybe she's just meant to be your muse?"

"Maybe. If so, she's doing a kickass job."

"She is."

"But she's also ruined me for other women."

"So it seems. But I am one hundred percent certain there's a real living and breathing muse in your future, Elena."

"I wish I could be as sure as you."

"We've had this conversation before and we'll probably have it again, but I am ever the optimist and a hopeless romantic. She's out there. Maybe in Seattle. Maybe in a land you have yet to visit. Maybe you'll walk right into her on the street. It always happens when you're not trying, so relax. Meditate if you want. But focus on your work, the gallery showing, and moving. I promise, if you focus on getting happy with the rest of the things in your life, great things will happen. It will all come together."

"Thank you, Marlie. You really are the best."

"Oh, I know. Even she can't compete with me," Marlie said with great stoicism.

Elena smiled at the comment. "No one can." She glanced between Marlie and the canvas, then said, "Let me clean up and we can go grab a bite."

"No rush. I'll be right here. I think her and I," she motioned between herself and the woman in the painting, "need to have a conversation."

Elena laughed out loud at the stern expression on Marlie's face paired with the idea of her talking to a painting. "Okay. Don't be too hard on her though. Wouldn't want to scare her away." She walked back to her canvas and picked up her brushes.

When Elena had disappeared into the backroom, Marlie faced the woman in the forest. Her mouth turned downward into a tight frown as she mulled over what to say. It was all very silly of course, speaking to a painting, but if Grandma Mai believed there was a real woman out there trying to find her way to her best friend, well then, it was worth a shot.

"You know, it's not right what you're doing to her." She paused as if a response were physically possible. Those blue eyes met her own without waver, almost intimidating in the power of their gaze. But Marlie would not be bullied—certainly not by an inanimate woman. "Elena deserves to be happy and you're keeping her from that. If you really love her, you'll either let her go or woman up and get your ass here so I don't have to find it and kick it."

A swift breeze filled the room. A chill zipped down her spine as her hair jumped on end. Marlie's head spun on a swivel in search of its origin. There was none to be found. She was alone and not a single window or door was open, yet the draft continued to bristle her skin. *Impossible.* Her head whipped back around, meeting the blue eyes of the painting once again. They were no longer hard. A light gloss covered them and Marlie nearly expected a tear to fall. Sadness radiated from the woman born of oils and brush strokes and the colors dulled, as if the very life of everything on the canvas was slowly draining into the ether.

"Elena," the breeze whispered, sounding more like a question than a confirmation. At least, that's what Marlie swore she'd heard.

Was that real? Should I answer? Oh heck, here it goes.

"Yes, Elena." Marlie stood tall and perched her hands on her hips. When it came to dealing with the spirit world, she hadn't a wisp of knowledge, but if this was her chance to make contact, she would be sure to speak her mind. "Elena Jake of Portland, Oregon. So, now you know where to be. I expect to meet you soon. Otherwise, let her go. It would hurt for a while, but at least she could move on. She could find the happiness and love she deserves. A real one. Someone that would hold her at night and nurse her when she's ill. Not one that leaves her feeling like shit every morning because she's alone. Hell, you're like my college ex, except I had to put up with him twenty-four-seven. Sure woulda been nice if he had had a disappearing act too."

This is so weird. God, I hope it works. "Anyway, that's all I have to say. What about you? Anything you want to say?"

The breeze swept over her once more and again she heard its wispy voice. "Elena Jake," it whispered in her ear like a soft song in the summer night air. Then it was gone.

"I'm all set," Elena called out from the doorway, none the wiser. "You ready?"

Marlie flinched at the sudden intrusion. She didn't answer right away. She couldn't. All she could do was stare at the painting before her. Had it all been her imagination? A minute was needed to process. And probably a bottle of wine.

"Did you two have a pleasant conversation?" Elena asked with a smile dancing in her tone.

Marlie jumped when Elena appeared by her side. The painting was just as it had been upon first sight—untouched, exploding with color, everything as it should be—but something was different about the stranger with the outstretched hand. Was that a hint of a smile?

"Umm, yes. Yes, we did," Marlie replied, hoping her voice didn't reveal how rattled she was on the inside. There was little to worry about though. Elena was too enamored with the painting to notice.

"You really love this painting, don't you?" Elena leaned in close, studying the face, then turned to Marlie.

Had she noticed the change as well? Could a physical change really even happen? Marlie's mind couldn't comprehend the possibility. Remembering Elena's question, she finally replied, "It's beautiful, Elena, and quite unique."

"Maybe I'll give it to you."

"No." Definitely no. Not after that experience. "I have a feeling this is one you should keep."

Elena shot her a perplexed look and chuckled as she moved her attention back to the canvas. Silence filled the room before she turned back and said, "Okay…well, I'm starving. Where should we go?"

"Anywhere with a full bar," Marlie replied. As they turned to leave, she glanced over her shoulder one last time. "I need something stronger than wine," she muttered under her breath and followed Elena out the door.

CHAPTER TWENTY-FIVE

Atlanta - Same Time

Tess glanced at the clock through hazy eyes. It was only four in the afternoon, but the fog had returned to her brain and her eyes had begun to hurt. There were signs that a headache was on the way. Napping in the afternoon made her feel like an old lady, but it was either that, or suffer in the name of foolish pride.

She closed her psychology journal and set it on the coffee table. Her hands came to rest folded neatly on her lap. Tess glanced down and admired her newly cast-free left arm. The skin was pale and flaky and the muscles atrophied, but it was sure nice be rid of it. She had more than enough reminders of that fateful day already.

"Evan, I'm going to lay down for a bit. Wake me for dinner if I'm not up, please?"

"Sure. Are you feeling okay?" he asked without looking up. His eyes skimmed across the computer screen as his fingers furiously typed away.

"Not too bad, but I can feel a headache coming. Must have been too much reading."

"And yet, you keep fighting the doc to let you on your tablet when you still can't handle magazines."

Wearing a proud grin, Tess shrugged. "You know me."

Evan stopped and turned his full attention to her. "I do and that's why I worry. But I also know you're a very intelligent woman, who despite wanting to race back into life, realizes her situation. You've been doing very well practicing patience."

"Thank you. You have no idea how damned hard it is."

He let out a boisterous laugh. "Just think of how much better you'll be able to help your clients once you've beaten this."

"Yeah. Sure. Thanks for the positive spin." Sarcasm painted her words as well as her expression, making sure Evan knew her true stance on his comment.

"Anytime." He smirked in return and then commenced typing again. "Be sure to drink some water before bed. We have to keep you well hydrated."

Tess stood at attention and delivered a half-hearted salute as she said, "Yes, sir." Evan chuckled as she strolled into the kitchen, filled her glass with water, and then chugged it to the last drop. "Water has been consumed, sir," she called out, then headed toward her room.

"Good girl," Evan returned with a snicker.

She rolled her eyes but grinned, appreciating his diligent care. At the base of the staircase, she paused to stare at a photo. It had been taken two days before Evan's twentieth birthday as their mom and dad were leaving on their fatal trip. The four of them stood in front of a small plane on a runway with arms over shoulders, their parents bookending her and Evan. Big smiles graced all four faces. If only she had known...surely, she would have said or done something different.

Her chest tightened and she fought back a tear. Some things never got easier. She so badly wished they were still here to help her through this now. "I miss you guys so damned much," she whispered and reverently touched the photo. With a heavy-hearted sigh, she ascended the stairs.

When she reached the second floor, she was winded. Her energy had drained with every step. The heaviness was new and scary. Perhaps this headache would be the worst yet. Naps had fended off the beast in the past, so she stuck to her plan and dragged herself to her room, passing out nearly as fast as she hit the mattress.

Tossing and turning, a bead of sweat rolled down Tess's forehead. A light breeze crept through her room, causing a shiver to rumble through her body. She groaned and rolled on her side, pulling her covers up to her chin.

Her eyes clenched shut, flinching at bright bursts of images flashing through her dream. Whites. Greens. Yellows. Trees. A river. A tan walled room. An older woman with short graying hair staring at her with hands on hips, a determined glare, and a steeled jaw. The angry-looking woman's mouth moved without sound.

Was this a lecture? About what? And who the hell was she?

The stranger continued to speak, but no words could be heard. Tess focused in harder, catching the line, "Elena deserves to be happy." Any further words from the woman faded away as Tess allowed the name to roll off her tongue. "Elena."

"Yes, Elena. Elena Jake of Portland, Oregon," the woman answered. "So, now you know where to be. I expect to meet you soon. Otherwise, let her go."

Tess was floored by the fact she had received a direct reply. Her scientific mind could not grasp the very unscientific phenomenon happening in that moment. Who was this woman and who was Elena Jake? Was Elena her voice? Or, was the new woman a messenger sent to help find the source? Would finding Elena stop any further invasion of her mind? Maybe she was really just losing it—her neurons falling victim to the irreparable damage that's forever affected the inner workings of her brain.

Her mind was on a downward spiral, that was the obvious explanation and clinically, Tess had serious thoughts of having herself admitted after this episode. It was so unexplainable, but so exceptionally real. Beyond her mind's perception though, her heart wanted to find Elena more than anything. And deeper yet, her soul felt as if it needed the woman more than her body needed air—a concept so foreign she would need a translator to explain.

Yet, Tess understood it all so innately. Five minutes ago, the idea of wanting someone so badly it hurt would be like trying to breath under water—she couldn't do it. Now, here she was, aching to meet the faceless woman behind the voice, the one who's passionate words had moved her like none other.

Tess's focus returned to the disgruntled woman at hand who had apparently still been talking. She concentrated, using her full attention to hone in on the woman's words once again.

"Anything you want to say?"

Me? Was she asking me?

The expectant look on the stranger's face gave her the answer she needed, however, all she could utter was a name. A name that would soon go with a face, if all went well. "Elena Jake."

Portland, Oregon. *I hope I remember this when I wake up.*

The breeze ceased and Tess shot up with a start. Every detail of the dream remained explicitly clear. She jumped from her bed and rushed to her desk. Despite doctor's orders, she turned on her laptop. The millisecond the screen had loaded, her fingers tapped wildly upon the keyboard—*Elena Jake Portland, Oregon.*

The web search seemed agonizingly longer than usual. Her patience wearing thin, she was midway to slapping the table in frustration when two links matching her request appeared.

Tess clicked on the first one, a seventy-year-old university president. Her gaze surveyed the image of a very professional-looking, gray-haired woman with blue eyes who had aged exceptionally well, but seeing the woman did nothing for her. Thank goodness. Not that she had an age limit or anything, but it would be weird to have a voice in her head of a woman twice her age, wouldn't it?

A laugh rolled out and she shook her head. Funny how things had changed. How weird was it to have any voice in her head at all and here she was judging the potential sources like an internet dating site? Tess chuckled again as she closed the page and moved on to the second link.

All laughter ceased, as did her breath, the moment the pixelated image became clear. Tess sat mesmerized, staring into the brown eyes of the artist's headshot. The eyes...she'd seen them before somewhere, somehow. They were comforting, sending a warmth throughout every cell. Her body signaled its approval with a racing pulse and an overwhelming desire for all things Elena Jake.

The warmth quickly gave way to pain. Her eyes wrenched shut as a searing ache ripped through her head and chest. Tess crumbled to the ground, groaning in agony.

Images flashed before her shuttered eyes. Two young girls in a heated moment. Heartbreak was the overwhelming emotion. Tess felt it to her core as if it were her own. She held a particular connection to the young girl named Abbie—hearing her thoughts, feeling her emotions, as if they were one being. Helpless to protest, the scene rolled forward like an old movie.

"You're really going through with this? What about us, Mary?" Abbie yelled. Her pain echoed through the trees, sending birds scattering. Shaky fingers dragged through her shaggy blonde hair and she pulled at the roots. The sting momentarily distracted her from the crushing of her heart.

Mary stepped closer, her hand reaching out as tears raced down her face at the speed of the mighty river beside them. Abbie stepped away. Her denial sent Mary crumbling to her knees. "I love you, Abbie, with all my heart, but I have to marry George."

"You don't have to do anything you don't want to do, Mary McGhee." The venom in Abbie's words and the glare in her now dark blue eyes left no mistaking her feelings on her betrayal.

"My father insists. Besides, where would we go? What would we do? We talk about this all the time and never has there been an answer. The world doesn't approve of our love. We would be outcasts." Mary tried to reason. "I can't…"

"You don't know that. You don't know anything outside of this damned old town," Abbie spat.

"Neither do you, Abbie," Mary returned with uncharacteristic harshness. She stumbled to her feet, her legs still shaking.

"But I know we'd be together," Abbie softened, eyes glistening, "and that's all that matters to me. I'd work five jobs if I had to. I'd do whatever it took to make it work."

"I know you would and I love you more for it."

"But not enough to leave with me."

"Abbie-"

"No, I get it, Mary. You've always been afraid...too afraid to follow your heart unless we were hidden away." Abbie rushed forward, crashing their bodies together and crushing their lips in a bruising, final, passionate kiss.

Mary gripped her tightly, holding on for dear life as if trying to gasp for one last breath before drowning. There was such desperation in that final moment, a silent pleading to be saved, but Abbie couldn't be Mary's savior. Not this time. Not when Mary had willingly swum so far from shore.

As much as she had always wanted to be Mary's hero, walking away would be all she could do and while future decisions were unknown, she was sure it would be the hardest thing she would ever do. There was no staying. No pretending to be the happy friend. No Mary.

Abbie ripped herself free and sprinted away, leaving Mary adrift in the tumultuous sea she had chosen to dive into. She didn't look back. She couldn't. That place, that ground beneath them that held so many of the best moments of her life, had forever been soiled.

Bursting through the front door of her house and racing up the stairs, Abbie ignored the angry, protesting shouts of her parents and dived face first onto her bed sobbing. The excruciating pain of broken dreams and a shattered heart made it painful to breathe. Was it possible to ever be whole again?

She rolled onto her side. The orange, blue, and pink rays of setting sun outside her window were a blur through tear stained lenses. As she slid her arm up under her head, something caught her sleeve. Abbie carefully grasped the perfect edge of a crisp white envelope and lifted it to her eyes. The handwriting was unmistakable. Tears pricked yet again and she shook her head in disbelief that there were any more to shed.

Torn didn't begin to describe her current state. Did she want to read the words that lie in wait inside? Of course. More than anything. Deep down, she knew they'd be words of love bravely expressed in ink in a way Mary never had the strength to carry out in life.

Sad really, that anyone would deny themselves what they so truly wanted because of what others thought or said. More devastating, was it being the person she loved more than anything.

Abbie had never cared. She had stood face to face with her detractors, took all they could dish out, and then carried on. Sure, life could have been easier, but for love, for Mary, she would endure it all. She just needed Mary to be as strong. But it was not to be and it hurt in unimaginable ways. Far worse than the scorching looks by her family and townspeople or any beating she had ever received. She had persevered because of her love. Now, that was gone.

For ten heartbeats, she considered leaving the letter unopened, but she wanted the memory of them together to end on a good note as much as Mary.

She reached for the owl on her bedside table and clutched it tight to her chest. Several deep breaths were needed before she found the strength to open the letter. Abbie set the owl on the bed beside her. Her fingers traced over her name beautifully etched by Mary's hand in black pen across the bright white paper. With a delicate touch, she opened the flap and pulled out a single page. After a moment of hesitation, she unfolded it and gathered a deep, steadying breath, then read the first line.

My dearest Abbie,

It was as if Mary had whispered the words ever so softly into her ear. Her heart warmed and then broke all over again, but Abbie choked back a sob. She steeled the dam that held back a mighty river of tears. Desperate to read what may possibly be Mary's last words to her, she soldiered through with a shuddering breath.

By the time you read this, you will be more than upset with me. Please believe that I never wanted this to happen. I am so very sorry I couldn't be stronger for you. For us. I am sorry I could not give you the happily ever after you so desired, but I have given you my heart. Make no mistake, Abigail Carter, that even though we may not be together, my heart will only ever be yours for the rest of my life, and the next ten, and then ten more after that.

I hope one day you can forgive me and that in at least one of those lifetimes we will find happiness together in some shape or form. I will think of you with only the fondest of memories and pray we meet again in my dreams.

May light and love follow you always.

With all the love I have to give,

Your Mary

The dam crumbled. Tears rushed down her face with the speed of the mighty Mississippi. Sobs wracked her body with the crashing force of Niagara. Each time she'd thought she had no more left to give, that she had managed to freeze her heart, the ice would melt and release a new flood.

As exhaustion claimed her, Abbie vowed that tomorrow she would leave Bryson City, North Carolina and Mary McGhee behind for good.

CHAPTER TWENTY-SIX

A half an hour later, Tess came to curled up on the floor with her head in her hands. Her body ached and her mind was mush, but one name lingered on the tip of her memory lying in wait for her recollection. "Mary," she said, releasing it into the ether.

Dr. Coleman had asked her about a Mary. She must have been dreaming of her while she was in a coma. She had so many questions. What was the connection between Elena Jake and Mary McGhee? What was her role in it all? Evan had mentioned she'd thought her name was Abigail Carter when she'd woken up. Was it the same Abigail Carter? It was too big of a coincidence to be any other. But what did it all mean? And why was it happening to her?

A breath of relief excitedly broke free as the shooting pain in her head dissolved. Strained muscles relaxed and her eyes fluttered open with caution. The computer stared down at her without judgement. Unsure of what her fate would be if she dared attempt to read the screen again, she couldn't *not* know.

She hurried to her feet, staggering from the quick change in position, then flopped into the chair. Her fingers moved fast across the keys. She paused for one more look into the soft brown eyes of Elena Jake before hitting enter. The search engine swirled, then pulled up one result for Abigail Carter and Mary McGhee. Her breath hitched and for a moment, she considered closing it and ignoring the entire thing.

But she couldn't. Something tore at her insides needing to be freed, or avenged, or reunited, or...Tess had no idea really, but whatever it needed, perhaps the quicker she got to the bottom of it all, the quicker she would resolve her problem.

Without another thought, she clicked the link and awaited the reveal. Her index finger tapped with impatience atop the wooden desk until an old black and white newspaper image appeared. The pages had been scanned in microfiche style. Tess zoomed in and slowly skimmed the front page.

June 30, 1954, *Bryson City Journal*. A chill penetrated her skin. She had been near Bryson City with Amy when she'd had that terrible episode. And June 30? That was the same day as her accident. More eerie facts that were too close to be a coincidence.

She shook herself free and continued the search. The big story of the day was hard to miss—a solar eclipse could be seen across the state. Hordes of people had flocked to the area to witness the event. A photo showed a large crowd holding up protective film as they stared up at the sky. In the bottom corner of the page was the Cherokee Fourth of July festival announcement. The next page was full of advertisements and socials, including a hometown hero who had married his high school sweetheart. The happy couple was pictured holding one another and smiling wide for all to see.

When Tess arrived at page three, her heart stumbled and her breath was ripped from her chest. Two pictures placed side by side, formal photos of young girls. There was Abigail, with her short, light-colored hair wearing a button-down shirt and pants, looking very boyish. Her eyes were intense and familiar.

Then there was Mary, demure and innocent, with long, curly hair wearing an ankle length dress with what appeared to be flowers. Above, the headline read "Two Bryson City Girls Die in Tragic Car Accident."

Though she had read the words, the need to repeat them, to say them aloud and cement them as reality was felt with unprecedented urgency. "Car accident." Again, a chill wracked her body, deeper this time, gripping her heart. A series of images scrolled in succession through her memory—the red hood of a vehicle against a stormy sky. The driver's side view of soaring off the edge of the cliff. Violent rolling. A scream. The smell of exhaust. An apology. Bloodied hands. Darkness.

With every image, the nausea and emotions Tess had felt the first time returned with a vengeance. "Not again," she whined to an empty, spinning room. She gripped the desk to keep from falling out of the chair. *"I'm sorry"* echoed in her head and thundered in her chest. She fought the bile rising in her throat and forced herself to read the brief story.

The two girls, Mary McGhee and Abigail Carter, both eighteen years old, had died when their truck lost control and fell over the cliff on Route 441 during the storm. Seemed Mary had fled her wedding to George Arlan Smythe. He had been in pursuit of Abigail's truck when the weather had taken a turn for the worst, and so had their fate.

Such a tragic event. Even had she not experienced the intimate hallucinations, her heart would have broken for them. How much more was there to the story? The feelings Tess had been privy to hinted at a very close relationship. Best friends? Perhaps even lovers?

A twinge shot through her chest at the thought, forcing her eyes closed and twisting her facial muscles into another painful grimace. A new image appeared, one of an owl carved in wood. A warm breath whispered against her ear, "May light and love follow you always." It was the sweetest voice she had ever heard and the southern accent soothed her like a warm bath. The words were familiar and stirred a longing she couldn't fathom.

The pain eased and once again, Tess sat in confused awe at the events taking place. A trip to that regression hypnotist could be in order, but regardless of the results, there was a power drawing her to Portland and Elena Jake.

Maybe the answers would be found there. The revelation awakened a sudden need to get across the country as fast as possible. She had to meet Elena. Every nerve, every muscle, every voice of reason screamed, "ACT NOW! GO TODAY!"

A burst of energy got her out of her chair, but then reality struck in the form of dizziness and nausea. She steadied herself on the desk again and took a breath. "Shit," she muttered and shook her head.

After taking a moment to settle, her mind and body calmed, but the urgency returned. She raced to the nightstand to retrieve her phone and quickly dialed Dr. Coleman. Her foot tapped with nervous anticipation of their conversation. Hopefully, he would answer. It wasn't the easiest thing in the world to get a doctor on the phone.

On the fourth ring, Tess let out a huff of frustration, but as she pulled the phone down to end the call, she heard his voice on the other end.

"Tess?"

"Um, hi. Sorry to bother you."

"Are you okay?"

"No, umm...I mean, yes, I'm fine, but I have an emergency in Portland and I need to get-"

"I won't clear you to fly. You're still having dizzy spells. You really shouldn't travel at all yet."

"I know, but I'm doing so much better. Can't you-"

"I'm sorry, Tess. You know I can't. If you really must go, you'll have to find another way. There's the bus, or maybe Evan can drive you."

Her body fell slack in defeat. "Okay," she said, hoping to keep the disappointment from her voice. "I understand."

"Good. I'll see you in two weeks."

"Yep." Maybe. There was no telling what would happen in Portland. "And thank you for everything you've done for me," she said and hung up before he could say another word.

Of course flying would be out of the question. She could hardly go from sitting to standing without symptoms. The changing pressure of elevation would be brutal and she would be stuck up there. She was in no condition to drive that far either, not when her eyes and the bright light of day had become mortal enemies. Besides, she would tire too quickly. She could ask Evan. On second thought, there was no way he was getting an explanation about her sudden need to hit the Pacific coast.

Tess let out a defeated groan and dropped her head. She flopped back into her chair, set her fingers to the keyboard, and looked up Amtrak. One hundred and eleven hours? She'd go mad before arriving. Apparently, there was no straight shot to Portland by train. In fact, she'd travel most of the country first.

She leaned back as another loud groan of frustration rumbled out. *Think Tess.* She ran her palms down her face, then leaned forward and typed again—*fastest way to get to Portland.*

A breath and a half later, the results were in. She chose the link that cited several options. A plane? That's out. Car? Nope. Absolutely not. Bus? Maybe, but three days cooped up like that in a tiny seat beside a stranger...last resort. Train? Way too long. But then she found her answer. It wasn't as good as she'd like, but it appeared to be her best solution. A combo bus with train taking two and a half days. She would take a bus to Chicago and then an AMTRAK to Portland. A bus ride that length wouldn't be too brutal and at least the train had actual beds and room to roam.

A five-hour flight would still have been preferred, especially with her single-minded push to get there, but circumstances were what they were. Besides, she hadn't seen North Dakota or Montana yet. The trip would either give her some time to try to make sense of things or drive her nuts from impatience. She'd find out soon enough.

The exhilaration of her upcoming adventure settled into her bones. She hadn't traveled by train since her parents had taken them to Europe when she was sixteen. There was a certain sexiness about moving car to car, watching the terrain change as each state came and went. Trains gave you a unique view of the cities and small towns, and a much better perspective than an interstate that was riddled with nothing but billboards and rest stops.

Their tracks had been laid way back when trains were the centerpiece of a town. Now, the world had grown like weeds outward, relegating them to something akin to a forgotten yard ornament allowed to become overgrown with weeds. You know it's there, but continue to ignore it, even as it peeks its head out from time to time when storms shift the brush or autumn claims the camouflaging leaves. Sad really, that something so beautiful, so life changing once upon a time, that still did so much for a country, could be discarded as nothing more than an annoyance when they sounded their horn or blocked traffic to pass.

Tess looked up at the wall and stared at the blankness of its off-white face. She didn't recall having such a fondness for trains before, but her heart embraced the idea of railcar travel, almost like taking a trip back in time. When Amy had proposed a train trip across Canada she had been averse to the idea.

Why the sudden change? Maybe it had been the prospect of being cooped up with Amy. No point in hashing it over now. Amy was gone and something had changed. Hopefully, Portland held the answers.

She slowly got to her feet to retrieve her wallet, then returned with renewed vigor. Several minutes later, she had booked the bus and train trips. Staring at the AMTRAK confirmation page, her head swam in disbelief, but her heart thumped in excitement. It felt right. Really, really right.

The bus would leave tomorrow at noon. She was ready to go right now, just a backpack and a wallet, but whatever journey lie ahead would have to wait. There was one more obstacle she had to overcome. She had to get past Evan.

CHAPTER TWENTY-SEVEN

Portland - Aug 21, 2017

As the train rolled into Union Station, Tess's body pulsed with a vibrancy she had never known. She wanted to focus on the sights of the city, but her mind raced with questions of where to start her search.

The fatigue of consecutive sleepless nights speckled with the image of Elena Jake seeped away. The anticipation of losing herself in those eyes sent a flow of energy down to her knee, making it bob up and down a hundred miles an hour. Her toes curled inside of her blue and white Nike sneakers. The wait for the signal to disembark felt like the longest of her life.

Tess reached up and adjusted the bun in her hair. She took a deep breath and rolled her neck to loosen muscles that had grown tight from sitting. Of course, the tension gripping her body brought on by days of suspense wouldn't help the process any.

She thought back to the morning of her departure. That was the last time she had heard from *Her*. The voice had mentioned a move to Seattle, which had only increased Tess's urgency, not to mention irritation, at having to take the long way to her destination. Was the woman even still in Portland? Tess had no clue and it was driving her nuts.

Tess groaned and vigorously dragged her palms up and down her face. The fact she hadn't heard another peep during the trip not only left her guessing, but it had been surprisingly unsettling. While the lack of migraines was definitely appreciated, she could admit she had missed the comforting, silvery tone and the mystery of what would happen next. This has been the greatest puzzle of her life and her analytical side was in heaven.

All other things considered, the trip hadn't been bad. The sleeper car accommodations were comfortable enough and the landscape had been breathtaking as she traveled along the northern United States through Fargo, Whitefish, Spokane, along the Columbia River, and past Mount Hood. Indian reservations and national parks, small towns and big cities, mountains and rivers. If it hadn't been for the raging desire spurring her anxiousness to get to Portland, the trip would have been quite enjoyable.

But then there was Evan, who had started calling one day in. Tess had answered him once, but had ducked him ever since. She'd have to speak to him soon though. There was no doubt he was worried, just as she would had the roles been reversed. Her fingers drummed away on the arm of her seat. Maybe now was a good time to call, then she would be free to do whatever she needed to do with a clear mind. Her decision made, she reached into her backpack and retrieved her phone.

"I'll sure miss this view."

Tess's head snapped up at the long-awaited arrival of the familiar voice. Every muscle froze. Her heart and lungs abandoned all work. The grip on her phone loosened and it fell to the floor, but she remained still, listening intently for the next words to come. Several painful seconds of silence had her begging the universe not to leave her hanging again.

"The Willamette River. The wharfs. The marketplace."

The return of the very first word enabled Tess to take a gasp of desperately needed breath. Her heart resumed its function, pumping strong and fast. The rest of her cells responded in kind. Her tight muscles attempted to relax, but failed. A gentle prodding started low in her belly, whispering a secret to her brain that she was not yet privy to, keeping Tess on edge.

"Dragon boats. Cherry blossoms at the waterfront in spring. Salmon Street Fountain. Seattle just won't be the same. Not as laid back. Too commercial. Too concrete. Too...something. It's not Portland, but change can be good, right?"

Were these clues? Was Elena near one of those landmarks now or was that where Tess was supposed to find the source of the voice? Were they one and the same?

Tess was still uncertain. After the episode with the older woman lecturing her, she had grown even more unsure, so Tess decided to let her gut lead the way. As soon as she was off the train she'd catch a cab and hope her subconscious nudge would take her to the source, or at the very least, to someone who could give her answers.

A ringing interrupted her thoughts. She glanced at her phone on the floor. Evan's name lit the screen. Sparked into action by the desire to get it over with, Tess picked up her phone and answered, "Hello, Evan."

"Tess, thank god! Where have you been? You said you were going home, but I haven't heard from you in three days. I was about to call the cops and file a missing person's report," Evan rambled on in a panic.

"Relax. I'm fine. I just needed to get away and you would have said no."

"You don't know that."

"Seriously, Evan?" Tess's brows shot up, knowing darn well he would have locked her in the house in order to keep an eye on her.

"Okay," he conceded with a long exhale. "You're right. But only because I know you won't take care of yourself properly."

"I'm good and I'll be back soon."

"Back?" The panic in his voice returned. "From where?"

Tess paused and considered whether or not to tell him the truth. After careful consideration, she had never lied to her brother before. Omission, on the other hand, she was definitely guilty of, but now wasn't the time to admit she had been hearing voices and followed them on a cross-country journey.

"Portland," she replied with hesitance. Hopefully, one day it would be a funny story over drinks.

"Oregon? What the hell, Tess? You didn't-"

"No, I didn't fly. I took the bus, then the train. It was a beautiful ride."

"Maybe I'll find you there. Or, maybe this will all fade away. Tomorrow starts a new journey and I can't decide if I'm terrified or excited."

Upon hearing *Her* again, Tess needed to refocus her full attention. Besides, it was nearly time to get off the train. "I'm sorry, Evan, but I have to go. I'll call you back later."

"What? Go where? What's going on? I'm com-"

Tess silenced him by ending the call. He would probably be out here tomorrow, but all that mattered was right now. There was something much more urgent she needed to tend to.

Finally free to leave the train, Tess grabbed her backpack, bolted from her seat, and exited as fast as she could. She nearly sprinted down the platform and out of Union Station to grab the first cab she could find.

"Where to?" the driver asked as she scrambled into the back seat.

"I don't know exactly, but can you drive down to the riverside? I'm meeting someone."

"Sure."

Tess was relieved he hadn't questioned her lack of specifics. She relaxed back in the seat and closed her eyes, silently requesting more details. Her heart raced at the realization that she could possibly meet the source. But could she really? It was unheard of and beyond anything she could imagine. The more likely truth was it had all been due to her injury. If she came up empty, she would return to Atlanta and seek treatment. She had hidden her secret too long already.

They turned onto Southwest Naito Parkway and the river came into view. Thousands of people lined the waterside park area, sending Tess into a panic. How would she find her now?

"What a perfect day for an eclipse."

Eclipse? That's right, today was the day. That would explain the masses. No wonder everything had been booked up. Tess had been too preoccupied to keep up with current events.

Like some mystical kind of magnetic attraction, she was suddenly blind-sided by the need to head for a giant fountain. "Is there a big fountain here somewhere?" she asked the driver.

"Yep. Salmon Street. Just up ahead."

"That's where I want to go."

As they approached, she skimmed the crowd. Her subconscious startled her with a scream of "STOP!" The urgent internal appeal spilled over into a verbal plea from her own mouth. "Stop here, please," she yelled, frightening the driver.

He slammed on the brakes. Tess's body jerked forward as she fumbled to pull money from her pocket. She tossed him a fifty, slung her backpack over her shoulder, and jumped out.

Left and right she scanned as she walked briskly down the sidewalk. In her head, a song played, growing louder the farther she walked, until a matching tune struck her eardrums.

This is new. She stopped and surveyed the crowd. Surrounded by hundreds of sky-gawking people, she spun in place. Disorientation set in as faces passed in a blur. When her eyes trailed past a flash of bright color, the music stopped. A quick glance revealed a bird tattoo on the left shoulder blade of a woman that was oddly familiar, but not enough to slow her hunt.

When she turned away to continue the search, the music resumed, the level of sound increasing the farther she deviated. Taking a clue from the change in volume, she spun back around until silence had engulfed her once again.

Tess's focus settled on the curvaceous figure of a tattooed woman in jeans and a black tank top. Her hair was dark and faded on the sides with the loose strands in the middle ruffled by the breeze. The red, blue, and yellow feathers of the fiery bird with blazing orange eyes almost seemed to shimmer under her inspection, entrancing her.

The woman stiffened, as if feeling her stare, then turned around in alarm. Wide, dark eyes and even darker hair highlighted her tanned skin. It was Elena.

"You?" she gasped in complete and utter astonishment.

The single word left Tess breathless. The voice was unmistakable. It had haunted her dreams and interrupted her days. It was *Her*. The very acknowledgement made Tess's heart skip, but also brought with it a sense of peace.

Staring at Tess in shock and awe, Elena approached slowly, disbelievingly. The wind kicked up as the moon consumed the sun. Face to face they stood. Elena gawked at her like a long-lost friend, but besides the familiar voice, Tess was at a loss to dig up any recognition. Still, the connection was undeniable, like she'd known the other woman her entire life. She had no words and no fathomable explanation.

"You're real." Elena blurted, still awestruck. Her hand reached up to touch Tess's cheek, but stopped inches away. Her forehead crinkled as if unsure what to do next. A gust of wind rustled her hair.

Tess's forehead crinkled as she analyzed the statement. "You know me?"

"I know your face."

"How?" Had she also heard voices? Was it possible she had already looked up Tess in a similar fashion?

A shy smile formed and Elena shook her head. "You'll think I'm crazy."

Tess couldn't tear her eyes away. "Try me."

"I've been dreaming of you for years."

"Dreaming?"

"Yes. I don't know why or how. My grandmother says we have a soul connection from a past life."

"Not long ago I would have thought it ludicrous, but the last few weeks…it's unexplainable. There's nothing in science or research that makes sense of what I've felt and heard. A stranger's voice in my head, your voice, steered me here," Tess took a deep breath, "and now, here you are," she breathed out, releasing the last of her anxiety.

"Here *we* are." Elena stepped closer, still admiring her face with reverence.

Tess nodded and threaded all ten fingers with Elena's, an instinct so natural she didn't even think twice despite just having met her. The first contact of skin on skin sizzled. Both looked down at their joined hands, then back up again, smiling as wide as the horizon and lighting all the way up to their eyes.

Everything about Elena felt right, like nothing Tess had ever felt for any other person before. That empty cavity in her chest had magically become full. Elena's deep brown eyes held no interest in anyone but her and she warmed from within.

Then, recognition struck. There was no mistaking the pair of eyes in the deep, rich shade of the finest dark chocolate, the ones that shone with such love that Tess melted when she looked into them. She had definitely seen those brown eyes before. They had belonged to Mary.

Her breath caught again. If Elena had been Mary, then…

Everything suddenly made sense. There was nothing scientific to be explained. This was bigger than science, bigger than anything she could wrap her head around. But understanding meant nothing when the proof was standing right in front of her. The realization comforted her in more ways than one and in that moment, the only words that summed up her feelings were relief and overwhelming completeness.

The smile on her face reached the very core of her being, honest and true, as she introduced herself, "Hi. I'm Tess."

∞ ∞ ∞

"Hi, Tess. I'm Elena."

"Hi," Tess said again. Her wide smile turned shy, pulling at pink tinged cheeks. "Elena," she repeated her name in a nearly breathless whisper.

Wordless, they stood staring into one another's eyes until Tess finally broke the silence. "I have so many questions."

"You and me both." Elena slid her left hand free. This time, when she reached up, she did cup Tess's cheek. The air around them crackled. A sharp hitch of breath and a flushed face let Elena know she wasn't alone in the magical moment. Unable to look away, Elena lost herself in the blue eyes she'd only seen in dreams or on canvas, though neither did justice to the real thing.

Oh yes, so many times she most certainly could have drowned in their ocean of bright blue, but she had kept swimming and here, now, she had finally reached the other side. She had no intention of letting this woman out of her sight anytime soon.

She ripped her gaze free to roam the rest of Tess's body. Loose fitting black jeans and a baggy blue T-shirt suited her lean form well, not to mention the way they made her eyes pop even brighter. Her dark hair was pulled back tight, contradicting the relaxed vibe of her clothing.

Elena decided she much preferred the long flowing hair she had always pictured. She noted the small scar above Tess's left eye. Elena thought she had memorized every detail, yet that had forever escaped her. What else had she missed? "Maybe we should start over a drink?"

"How about a coffee?"

"Perfect. I know just the place."

With their fingers entwined, they strolled through the crowd. No words were needed, though there was so much to learn. But questions could wait. For the next six blocks, just the physical presence of Tess had calmed the twenty-plus year internal war that had waged within Elena. She wasn't crazy after all. Those blue eyes were very real and she quite literally had just met the woman of her dreams.

Most of all, Elena's soul felt as if it was finally whole. There was no doubt in her mind that Tess had been Abbie. Not with those unmistakable eyes. And she found comfort in the realization that she had been Mary, who had loved Abbie with all her heart. It was no wonder the woman had had such a strong hold on her all those years.

Their bodies drifted closer, shoulders bumping as if they'd always been together. The sun reclaimed its glory and the wind died down to a gentle breeze. Like the Earth and Halley's Comet, whose paths hadn't crossed in far too many years, their long journey back to one another had come to an end.

CHAPTER TWENTY-EIGHT

Hand in hand, they stepped through the door of a crowded diner and Tess froze when her eyes landed on a familiar face working behind the counter. Elena was yanked backward by Tess's anchored feet when her arm reached the end of its length.

She walked back and whispered, "What's wrong?"

Tess was about to reply, but then those amber eyes met hers and it was as if she was back in that dream.

CRASH!

Tess never flinched at the sound of broken glass. Her eyes remained locked on the familiar woman with short graying hair, but Elena spun around. Marlie stared at them in a shocked stupor. The crowd silenced for a brief moment, then returned to their lives without a care. Elena's eyes darted between Marlie and Tess several times over before giving Tess's hand a tug.

Her feet unearthed themselves and she shuffled forward, following Elena's lead toward the other woman who had moved to the open end of the counter. Tess's heart thumped like crazy, vibrating into her throat. She'd never been so nervous and prayed she wouldn't pass out, but despite the anxiety, she actually felt better than she had even before the accident. Elena brought them to a stop three feet away from the shell-shocked woman.

"Wow, um…" Marlie stuttered. "Wow."

"I know," Elena said and turned to smile at Tess. "Marlie, I'd like you to meet Tess."

"Wow," was all she could say again.

"That's pretty much all I have to say too," Tess agreed, then cleared her throat and held out her hand. "Hi, Marlie. It's nice to meet you in real life."

Marlie finally shook herself free of her daze and raised a brow, then smiled at the comment. She accepted the handshake and said, "I will say the same for you. More than you can imagine."

"I'm confused," Elena said, her face scrunched as she glanced between the two of them.

"You can thank Marlie for getting me here." Tess offered a soft smile. She adjusted her backpack, then reached down and took Elena's hand back in her own, basking in how perfect it felt.

"Story for another time," Marlie brushed any explanation aside. "But you're both welcome," she added with a wry grin.

"Okayyyyy…" Elena trailed off.

"Well, I'll be. The power of the trifecta came through. The universe does amazing things." All three turned to an old Indian woman with a thousand-watt smile that crinkled the lines up to her eyes. She stood in the doorway with her arms splayed open wide. "I knew my granddaughter was special. I told you so, didn't I?"

Joy emanated from her entire being and Tess couldn't help but feel comfortable in her presence. Marlie nodded, still seemingly speechless over Tess's appearance.

"You sure did, Grandma," Elena smiled and rushed to swallow the old woman in a warm hug. Her grandmother whispered into her ear. When Elena pulled away, her face was tinged with a blush, but her smile was wide and honest. "Mai, I'd like you to meet Tess. Tess, this is my grandmother, Mai."

Tess extended her hand but was swept into a tight embrace that lifted her to her toes. "Nice to meet you," she croaked out with what little breath she could muster. The old woman was surprisingly strong.

"So lovely to meet you, Tess." She finally released her hold, allowing Tess to regain her breath. Mai reached around, took Elena's hand, and placed it back into Tess's. "I am overjoyed to see these two souls reunited. This is truly a once in a..." She thought deeply about her next words. "Oh hell, it's more than a once in a lifetime opportunity. Maybe ten lifetimes. Probably even way more than that." She laughed and shook her head. "Anyway, I feel blessed to have witnessed it and I wish you much happiness this time."

This time. The words rattled around Tess's mind. Mai truly believed in the past life theory and somehow it made all the weirdness seem a bit less weird. How many people suffering from "mental illness" were actually experiencing the very same thing as she?

The question opened a whole new realm of possibilities to her clinical thinking and she had to ask, "Mai? What might have happened if we hadn't found one another? Or, if one of us had died first?" The last two words left a bitter taste in her mouth knowing how close she had come. Then there was Rod and Mariana. There was no doubt in her mind that they had been in the same situation, but with a sad result.

"I'm afraid I don't really know the answer to that, but like yin and yang who search relentlessly for their other half, I imagine it would be a sad and restless life. Or worse." She left it at that. The four of them remained silent as the sentiment hung over them, then Mai smiled and patted Tess on the back. "But we don't have to wonder about that, because here you are. And where did you come from? Sit. You must be hungry."

She hadn't thought about food much, but now that Mai had mentioned it, her stomach gurgled with excitement. "I could eat and I'm from Atlanta."

"All the way from Atlanta? Quite the trip. Well, we will let you two get acquainted, right Marlie?"

"Um, yes we will. What can I get you to drink?"

Marlie still stared at her with disbelieving eyes. Had Tess not been through all she had, she would have done the same. "I'll have a coffee, black please."

"The usual," Elena said. When Marlie and Mai had gone, she looked around until she spotted a free table. She waved her hand in its direction and asked, "Shall we sit?"

Tess smiled and nodded. She motioned for Elena to go first and when they reached their destination, Tess pulled the chair out for her. Elena flashed a soft smile as she settled herself. Tess swooped around to the other side, set her bag down, and sat across from Elena. She propped her elbows on the table top and set her chin in her hands.

Following a moment of comfortable silence looking into those dark brown eyes, Tess sighed. Her journey had come to an end. Warmth swelled in her chest and spread to her limbs, lighting her face with a genuine smile straight from her soul. "So, Elena, tell me everything."

∞ ∞ ∞

After a two-hour lunch filled with the usual small talk—where they were born, what they did for a living, and so on—Elena was ready to stretch her legs. She sensed Tess wasn't the sitting around type either. A trip to her warehouse studio seemed in order before they got much further along. The many pictures of Tess would either scare the woman away for good or cement that they were a love written in the stars.

A short walk to the Max light rail and a ten-minute ride later, Elena stood with keys in shaky hands poised to open the studio door. Her heart beat at breakneck speed. Tess smiled and placed her hands over Elena's to steady them. The warmth was soothing, calming her frantic pulse, though her mind still raced with fear.

"Relax," Tess comforted in a low tone. "I'm sure your work is beautiful."

Red flushed her cheeks and Elena glanced at her feet before looking up and replying, "Thank you, but it's the subject of my work I'm afraid of."

Tess furrowed her brow, pulling her scar downward. Elena had resisted asking about it over lunch, but she couldn't help wondering how she'd gotten it or how long it had been there? Was it related to the reason she'd recently had a cast on her arm? But those were questions for another time.

First, we have to get through this.

"Okay, so...here we go." Elena blew out a heavy breath as she slipped the key in. With the flick of her wrist, the door unlocked and swung open. She reached inside and turned on the lights. "After you," she said softly, then stood back and allowed Tess free rein of the room.

Tess took three steps in, then stopped. Her backpack dropped to the ground with a thump as her eyes traversed the row of canvases on display. Elena's body trembled as Tess remained still and the silence went on longer than she could stand. Finally, Tess moved toward the left, growing closer and closer to a row of brightly colored oil paintings. She came to a halt in front of the forest scene that had enamored Marlie. That was a popular one. Elena had to admit it was among her favorites too.

She wanted to give Tess space, but it was too hard to stay away. Elena moved quietly until she was at Tess's side. She took in every changing expression and shift in emotion as they struck Tess, wishing she could read her mind. The woman hadn't run yet, so that was a great sign. That thought allowed Elena a much-needed breath.

"This..." Tess breathed out in awe.

Elena's stomach dropped. She knew it. It was all too much. Tess was going to run for her life, she was sure of it. Elena prayed she'd be wrong. She grew dizzy as her breath held in wait of Tess's verdict.

"This is magnificent," Tess gushed. "So detailed, so real, so much feeling. You captured me and my feelings these last few weeks without ever meeting me. There are no words. Simply amazing." A wondrous, proud smile was on her lips when she turned to look at Elena.

"Thank you." Elena relaxed into an easy smile. "And thank you for not freaking out."

Tess returned her hand to Elena's. She laughed loudly and shook her head. The musical sound made Elena's belly flip in the most wonderful way. Her heart was so full it exploded onto her face, so much so, that her cheeks ached. The need to reach out and pull Tess close was rampant, but all she could do was stare, for if she gave in to her desire, Elena was certain she would lose all control.

She had waited for this woman for so long and with her now standing before her in the flesh, the pull was otherworldly. Elena mentally chided the spirits for forcing her to conjure up goddess-like self-discipline when she was just a mere mortal.

"How long did you say you've been seeing me?" Tess asked, shaking Elena from her internal back and forth.

"Seems like forever really, but ever since I was a little girl you've been visiting me." What once would have been an awkward confession, now seemed as normal as gray days in Portland.

Tess uttered a "wow" and returned to the painting. "I've seen this before, sort of." She cocked her head right, then turned around and took in the plain tan walls of the room.

"How?"

Tess shrugged. "Marlie lectured me from this spot," she explained, ending with a laugh. "She told me your name and here I am. I have no idea how it all works."

Elena knew exactly what day that had been. Once again, her best friend had come through for her in the biggest of ways. "Me neither." Elena shook her head. Their journey would never be fully explained, but she wasn't going to complain. The time for analysis was over. Now, she just wanted to enjoy it. "But I will never be able to repay her for that."

"Same here." Tess glanced down the row of canvases and said, "Seems you like my hair down." She turned to fully face Elena. Her hands swept up and released her long dark locks from their prison. She sifted her fingers through them as they flowed down over her shoulders and along the angle of her face, making her eyes appear even more blue against their dark frame. Her gaze raked the length of Elena from head to toe, then settled back on her eyes.

Elena swallowed hard. Was she in a dream? *I better not be.* Under Tess's attentive stare, Elena's heart drummed at a rate that rivaled a death metal tempo. Heat simmered between her legs and rose to the top of her head. Every muscle knitted into knots. Since the moment she had laid eyes on Tess, all she had wanted to do was kiss her blue-eyed dream girl, to feel the warm, supple, real life lips against her own.

Unable to fight the attraction any longer, Elena moved closer, stopping when they were mere inches apart. Shimmering specks of gray swirled in those beautiful blues that she'd never noticed before. Tess didn't rebuff her invasion of personal space and she breathed a soft breath of relief. Elena's focus fell to the tip of Tess's tongue as it slipped out and moistened her lips.

Elena could take no more. Her approach was the epitome of restraint. The need to crash their mouths together in a rush of molten need was strong, like a bull desperate to erupt from the gate, but she prevailed. This was one moment not to be ruined by feverish haste.

Her diligence was rewarded. Every second moved at the pace of minutes as her lifelong dream came true. Pink lips met her arrival with controlled hunger. The world fell away. Every dream, every fantasy, every possible adjective Elena's imagination had ever conjured up to describe the feel of those lips on hers failed to live up to the real thing.

They moved together, softly at first. Elena's hands slid through Tess's loose hair and her hips were gripped tight in return. The pace quickened and their hunger grew. Tongues danced. Mouths melded. Bodies molded. Gasps for air filled the room. When they teetered on the edge of devouring one another, they slowed again, sharing small, explorative kisses and gentle caresses.

Tess tentatively broke their lip lock, pulling back just enough to stare at Elena with darkened, love-filled eyes. "Amazing," she croaked out, then smiled and dipped her head to rest her forehead against Elena's.

"Yes," Elena agreed. She struggled to catch her breath, but kept a firm hold on the woman in her arms.

"Oh, sorry, umm…I just…"

The man's voice startled them apart. Elena whipped around and found Derek averting his eyes. She laughed. "It's all right, Derek. We're decent."

∞ ∞ ∞

Tess only had eyes for Elena and she silently cursed the man for ripping her from her arms. That kiss had been soul shattering. Her body had exploded upon impact and while her mind had been mostly empty, allowing her freedom from analyzing everything, she'd swore she'd gotten a flash of a smiling Abbie and Mary standing hand in hand. All felt right in the world.

With what she already felt for Elena, it became abundantly clear why she could never give Amy, or anyone else, her whole heart. It had always belonged to the woman with the warmest deep brown eyes she'd ever seen. Tess didn't give a damn what had happened before or how it all came to be now. This time, she would move heaven and earth to get their happily ever after.

"Oh, wow!" Derek exclaimed so loudly it echoed off the walls.

Tess flinched. Only then did she realize Elena and Derek had been talking while she had zoned out. She began a quick analysis of the stranger as if he were a client. His splattered blue overalls indicated he was most likely a painter as well and his vibe seemed to fit. The blond man-bun, however, seemed out of place. She would have pegged him as more the rugged, big beard type in an attempt to hide his boyish looks.

"That's your muse." Upon recognition, his eyes took Tess all in, but not in a creepy way. He seemed as in awe as she and Elena had been at first glance. "I was beginning to think I'd never get to meet her."

"Me neither," Elena added under her breath, just enough for Tess to hear.

Tess repressed a chuckle. Craving the return of Elena's touch, she threaded their fingers back together.

"This is Tess. Tess, meet my good friend and fellow artist, Derek."

"Nice to meet you, Derek." Tess said.

"Really good to meet you too, Tess." He looked back at Elena and said, "You never have her here to pose for you. I was always amazed at how much detail you got just going from memory." He glanced down at their intertwined hands. "But now I guess I know why." His brows bounced for emphasis and a wide grin filled his face as his eyes darted between them.

So, Derek wasn't in the loop. Oh, if he only knew.

"Anyway, carry on ladies. I just needed to grab a few things. Great to meet you, Tess. Maybe we can all grab a beer sometime?"

"Maybe," Elena answered in a questioning tone.

"That would be nice," Tess said. She was here now and wanted to get to know Elena's world—all of it.

"Great." He smiled, then retreated to the back corner where a tool box sat. Within a minute, he was gone.

They were alone again. The temptation to resume their activities swirled relentlessly. But not here. Tess didn't want another interruption. Still, she couldn't help placing another quick, chaste kiss upon Elena's extremely kissable lips.

She smiled as she pulled away. Elena remained in place with her eyes closed and a content smile, so Tess kissed her again, as if making up for their sixty-plus-years apart.

"I'm not opposed to you doing that all day," Elena muttered in a daze. Her eyes fluttered open. A mischievous twinkle shone in pools of warm brown.

"I'll keep that in mind." Then, betraying her intentions, Tess yawned. *Traitorous body.*

"It's been an overwhelming day, huh?"

Tess nodded, then added, "I just got in this morning."

"My goodness. What time was your flight?"

"I came on a train."

"A train?"

"Yeah, um. I had an accident a few weeks back." She pointed to the scar on her head. "I can't fly yet."

"Oh." Warm fingertips applied a gentle caress to the area and Tess melted into the touch. "Maybe we should call it a day and get you some rest. Where are you staying? I'll take you there."

Tess froze. She wasn't ready to end their evening, but she also hadn't booked a place yet. All her usual hotel choices had been full due to the solar eclipse and in her haste to get here, that detail had fallen by the wayside. "I hadn't booked anything yet. The trip was very last minute."

"A room is going to be hard to find today, but you're in luck. I know just the place."

"You do?"

"Mhm. I have an extra room."

"I couldn't." Truthfully, she wanted nothing more, but she didn't want to rush anything. "We just met and-"

"Seriously, Tess?" Elena laughed. "Really, it's fine. Besides, now that I finally have you in my clutches, I'm in no hurry to let you go."

"How can I argue with that?" Not that she would. Hearing that Elena was already every bit as attached as she was had her belly performing somersaults in excitement.

"I'd prefer you not even try."

"Lead on."

CHAPTER TWENTY-NINE

Elena covered Tess with a blanket, taking care not to wake her. Though it was only ten thirty, Tess had succumbed to her fatigue. The long trip, hours of conversation, and a carb-filled pizza and garlic knots dinner would do that to a person.

Elena sat on the edge of her oak coffee table and stared at the woman sleeping peacefully on her oversized couch. Her eyes drifted to the mole above Tess's brow and then up to the scar.

The story of her near fatal accident weighed heavily in Elena's chest despite the fact Tess was alive and well. Knowing how close she had come to losing her before they'd ever met stung deeply. She could feel the painful emptiness in her chest with just the thought and Elena thanked the spirits she didn't have to suffer through that experience.

Shifting from her own discomfort, Elena focused on what Tess must have gone through. Almost dying, then hearing voices and probably fearing she'd gone crazy must have been a horrifying ordeal, especially given her profession. As sad as it was that her world had gone through such upheaval, Elena couldn't feel bad at all. Maybe she was being selfish, but she didn't care. Her one wish had finally come true. Tess was alive and with her. They had kissed—an amazing, heart stopping kiss—and she looked forward to what tomorrow held for them.

Adding the stories of Tess's experience to her own, combined with what she had learned from Mai, was beyond mind boggling. Even though she had woken up day after day hoping it would be true, the fact remained it was all far too fantastical to happen.

Or, so she'd thought. She'd never been so happy to be wrong in her life.

Everything felt new and in sync with Tess's unexpected arrival—like the one thing she had needed to make sense of her world was the woman sleeping soundly on her couch. To her delight, Tess had echoed the sentiment. Many of the feelings Tess had described in past dating experiences had put Elena's life into perspective, such as why she had never been happy with any of her previous girlfriends. But what would happen now?

There was no way she was going to move to Seattle, but they still lived on opposite ends of the country and barely knew one another. Was there a dating protocol for reunited soul mates?

Mai probably had a book for that. Elena chuckled to herself. She took one more long look at Tess. Unable to help herself, she leaned forward and kissed her on the cheek. "Sleep well," she whispered.

Elena reached across and turned off the lamp. She stood and walked across the room to her phone on the kitchen island, flipping on the nearby light before she sat on a barstool. A missed text from Marlie grabbed her attention. No doubt her best friend wanted an update on her day with her dream woman.

When she swiped the message open, she smiled at how correct she had been. A million responses flittered through her mind, but in the end, she kept it short. *It was even better than the dream.*

Elena pressed send and couldn't help her smile. It had only been hours, but she and Tess seemed to click in all the right ways. Their view of family, values, and ethics all seemed to align. They both enjoyed a wide range of music, movies, and book genres. The outdoors was something they wished they saw more of and both had vowed to make it happen, starting with a hike tomorrow.

The mixed background of science and art between them left enough differences to be interesting. Tess asking Elena to refrain from singing in the car unless she could truly carry a tune made her laugh. At first, she had teased she could never deprive friends and loved ones of her musical talent and belted out a terribly off-key chorus of her favorite country song, but the look of horror she received had her agreeing to the request. While she could hold a decent tune, it wasn't something she did often, though she'd bet Tess wouldn't hold her to it if she did sing a bit here and there.

Their main disagreement had been coffee preference. A quiet chuckle refused to be held in when she recalled how passionately Tess had felt that coffee should only be consumed black. Well, Tess would have to get over it. Elena had no intention of changing. Thinking of coffee, her stomach cried out for one of its favorite pairings—donuts.

Her eyes scrolled across the kitchen counter to the Voodoo Donuts Marlie had left behind. She licked her lips in anticipation as she opened the pink box and skimmed the selection; Maple bacon, plain, Portland cream, and the Old Dirty Bastard with its chunky Oreo, chocolate, and peanut butter topping. Then, her two favorites, the Voodoo Doll and double chocolate cake. With six to choose from, she had narrowed it down to two, but it was hard to choose between the double chocolate cake or the Voodoo Doll.

Her craving for the jelly was the decision maker. The Voodoo Doll's raspberry filling was to die for—a funny thought considering she had just bitten into a doughy, red jelly-filled donut man. She shot another quick text thanking her best friend for the treats. They'd come in handy in the morning too.

Elena stuffed her mouth with another giant bite of donut. A satisfied groan slipped free and a dab of jelly leaked out. It dangled at the corner of her mouth awaiting rescue. A laugh filled the room. Her head whipped toward the couch. A wave of intense embarrassment welled within when she found a pair of half-lidded, sleepy blue eyes watching her.

Elena quickly wiped her face with the back of her hand, then cringed at her lack of etiquette. She hoped she didn't look as mortified as she felt. With her cheeks still swollen full of donut, she rushed to chew as fast as she could. Tess only laughed harder.

"Stop it," Elena grumbled through her full mouth. It was hard to chew while suppressing a laugh of her own.

"Come here." Tess lazily lifted an arm and waved her over.

Elena moved slowly, making sure to swallow down the rest of her food by the time she arrived at Tess's side. Tess waved her down closer. When she bent over, Tess wiped the corner of her mouth.

"You missed a little," Tess said with a grin.

Elena's cheeks grew red. The heat of embarrassment warmed her face.

"Good donut?" Tess asked.

Her eyes were still sleepy, but they twinkled with something Elena couldn't place. They were almost smiling, yet held a desire that sent a shiver of excitement racing through her. "The best." Elena swallowed hard. "You want one?"

"Maybe later," Tess replied. She took Elena's hand and pulled her down until she was lying on top, breast to breast. "Is this okay?"

Was she serious? Elena beamed as she replied, "Very okay."

Tess's blues lit up. She settled herself underneath, then gently ran her fingers through Elena's hair, brushing it back from her forehead. Elena's eyes fluttered shut at the tenderness of the contact.

"You're so beautiful," Tess whispered with reverence, then touched their lips together in a soft, brief kiss.

Electric. That's what their kisses felt like. The paralyzing sensation lit Elena up and left behind a hum that set every cell in her body at attention in the most addictive way. A jolt so strong it was difficult to disconnect from its source. It took a moment for her brain to restart so she could choke out a faint, "So are you."

Their eyes locked and a million unspoken words were exchanged. Tess seemed unfazed by the intimate moment, lost in both her thoughts and Elena's eyes. Breaking the silence, but not their gaze, Tess said, "It's weird that I've never met you, but I feel like I've missed you forever."

Elena nodded as if she understood, but she didn't. How could she? She had seen Tess nearly every night for years. Instead of missing, she had yearned. She had ached to feel her touch, to look into her eyes, to feel the connection between them— everything that was now literally in the palm of her hands.

"Since the moment I saw your picture on my laptop," Tess breathed deeply, "something changed. I didn't even question it. And I usually analyze everything." She chuckled.

Tess's look of adoration was awe-inspiring. Elena shifted her weight for comfort. Her hand mindlessly caressed the skin of

Tess's arm and she remained quiet, allowing Tess to continue her train of thought.

Following her lead, Tess's hand began light circles across Elena's back as she spoke again. "So many things in life leave me with questions, to the point that I've made a life of trying to answer them. But not this. I feel like you and I are the most unquestionable thing I've ever known."

Tess brought both hands up to cup Elena's face. Her thumbs passed softly across Elena's cheekbones. "I may have only just met you, oh…" she tipped her wrist and glanced at her watch, "twelve hours ago, but I feel like I've known you forever. Is that how you feel?"

A lump in her throat kept Elena from doing anything other than nod. The moment was so surreal and so much more than she ever could have dreamt.

Tess pulled her down. Their lips met yet again with the same electrifying tingles of excitement, only this time, with heightened intensity. Tess's arms snaked around her in a possessive hold Elena wished would never be broken. Her mouth was consumed in a way that left no question she was being claimed.

Her heart overflowing with happiness, Elena gave herself freely, melting into Tess and allowing her to take whatever she wanted.

∞ ∞ ∞

The words had flowed out of Tess's mouth, speaking from a depth of her soul she didn't know existed. They were honest and true and unleashed an uncontrollable hunger for the woman in her arms. She wrapped her up like a python, pulling Elena as close as their cotton and denim barrier would permit.

It wasn't enough.

The kiss, meant to be gentle and sweet, was anything but. Their lips crashed together with bruising contact, sending a spark that ignited Tess's entire body. Her tongue demanded entrance and quickly received a warm, velvety greeting. A whimper of approval accompanied Elena's hips pressing harder into her own.

This hadn't been her intention when Elena had laid down, but she was powerless to stop it now. The need burning inside of her was primal and given Elena's response, it was mutual.

Tess gripped the bottom of Elena's tank top and pulled it up, breaking their lip lock only long enough for it to pass over her head. Dizzy and breathless, a quick gasp of oxygen was inhaled as Elena raised herself up. When she flopped back down and hungrily recaptured Tess's lips, all air was lost again.

The feel of Elena's soft, heated skin beneath her fingertips brought with it an intoxication like no other. Nimble fingers unsnapped the bra and slid the straps down. Without breaking the kiss again, Elena yanked it out from between them. Tess allowed her palms to freely explore the dips and curves of her lover's back until the rest of her body protested their special privilege.

A grunt accompanied Tess's weak effort to sit up. Elena was just as lost in passion and Tess needed a second attempt to get her intention across. Through heavy-lids, smoldering dark eyes devoured her without a touch. Swollen, half-parted lips trembled. A rush of want had Tess scrambling to get undressed.

Elena not-so-smoothly rolled across her and got to her feet. A soft smile held her lips as she extended her hand. Tess stood mesmerized as she got her first look at the full breasts and curvy hips that awaited her worship.

She snapped back to attention and accepted the outstretched hand. Without a word, Elena led her down the hall to her bedroom. A neatly made queen-size bed sat in the center. The green and blue comforter was a splash of color in the light gray room.

Elena turned and carefully pulled the shirt over Tess's head. With no bra to remove, she paused to take in the sight of her small, pert breasts erect with arousal before making eye contact as she undid Tess's jeans.

Cool air hit Tess's legs as her pants hit the floor, but warm hands came to rest on her hips. They blazed a heated trail to the center of her stomach, then up to her breasts. Elena massaged her sensitive flesh. The touch was so gentle, so loving, and the look in Elena's eyes...Tess had never felt so wanted in her life.

When they sank into the soft pillow top bed, flesh to flesh for the first time, Tess's body sang in relief. The purity of their love was enough to make her break into tears. Elena's fingers were magical and when they finally entered her slow and deep, every doubt she'd ever had of her inability to love another was wiped clean.

Every tender touch, every moan of approval, was memorized. Perhaps it would become a moment of recall in another lifetime, but this time, it was the pinnacle of fulfillment. A promise made and kept—ten lifetimes and ten more after that.

As Elena brought her to the edge of bliss and she gave herself over to the powerful eruption within, there were no more thoughts, only feelings, and that feeling was *Home*.

EPILOGUE

Bryson City, North Carolina - June 30, 2018

It was hard for Tess to believe it had only been a few hours since she'd stood across from her soon-to-be-wife dressed to the hilt. A black, short peak lapel tuxedo suit over a dusky blue waistcoat and matching cravat—Elena's request, saying it highlighted her blue eyes—was punctuated by her black and white wingtips. Holding Elena's hands in hers, she had stared lovingly into a pair of shimmering eyes that had taken on the same deep brown shade as the river running beside them. The backdrop of the sun's rays gleaming off the water of Tom Branch Falls was spectacular, but couldn't begin to compare to the beauty of Elena in a white taffeta wedding dress.

Tess had never seen her in a dress, but boy did she wear it well. Very well. Her wife, bold with her tattoos on display and beautiful with her curvaceous figure, could wear the feminine sweetheart strapless dress with the best of them. The neckline plunged to her cleavage, elegant, yet daring. Delicate lace patterns lined the waist accentuating her voluptuous form and pleats gathered on one side of the floor-length gown. Her dark hair, still cut into a fade along the sides, was done up with a pompadour down the center. The natural tan of her skin and her dark features stood out against the white fabric.

When the final "I do" had been said, the pace of Tess's heart accelerated, beating faster than the speed of sound until all that could be heard was a constant "whooshing" in her ears. Then, their lips met—their first kiss as a wedded couple. Everything ceased to exist outside of the two of them. There was no sound, no gushing guests, no river. The wind rose up, tickling her cheek, and a feeling of utter relief filled her being.

They had made it. They were married.

A calm washed over her and she sighed into the kiss, as did Elena. They broke away smiling. The air around them sizzled, filling Tess with indescribable energy. From the look in Elena's eyes and the vibrant aura surrounding her, it had affected her as well.

"Did you feel that?" Elena asked in a whisper.

"I did. And wow," Tess whispered back, her eyes still locked with Elena's. There was a new shine to those beautiful browns. She reached up and cupped Elena's face in her hands.

Elena's smile grew, as did the amount of blood rushing to her cheeks. She wiped a smudge of lipstick from the corner of Tess's mouth. "Yeah, wow."

"I think they approve."

"Me too."

With one more glance accompanied by joyous grins, they finally turned to the small gathering of family members and acknowledged their congratulatory whoops and hollers.

The vows, the dress, the kiss, the emotions…all memories locked forever in slow motion with every detail noted to the fullest. Everything that followed had passed in a blur, but their unconventional wedding plans had unfolded perfectly.

The private sunrise wedding in Smoky Mountain National Park had been followed by a brunch buffet reception for the rest of their friends at Mountain View Cabins, complete with chocolate fountain and a decadent half chocolate, half vanilla torte wedding cake. They shared their first dance to Brandi Carlile's "The Story," and at noon, the contingent of forty sent them off on their honeymoon in a topless green Jeep Wrangler with a "Just Married" sign affixed to the spare tire.

Having decided on a log cabin honeymoon in the mountains, they were excited to find Mountain View not only had an event pavilion, but also hosted three very secluded cabins. Elena had joked that it was perfect because they wouldn't have to wait long to consummate their marriage.

A rush of heat flushed Tess's cheeks as she recalled just how swiftly her wife had gotten her out of her suit when they had arrived. The flush grew redder as her body acknowledged it wouldn't mind a repeat now instead of trekking off for a late afternoon picnic. But they had a plan. The wedding date, honeymoon site, and trip to the riverside had been purposely chosen and were goal-specific in their intent—reverse karma.

The idea of battling unknown, mystical forces sounded daunting to Tess, though to Elena and Mai, it seemed as easy as returning an unwanted item at Walmart. Was there really anything they could do to affect future lifetimes? If they'd had more than one past journey together, had they always met undesirable ends? Would they truly get to enjoy their happiness in this life or would their fate forever be inevitable as that of star-crossed lovers?

Looking at Elena, feeling the depth of the emotions—wonderful, happy emotions—bubble from deep within until they escaped in the form of a smile, a kiss, a tear, or an "I love you," it didn't matter. Nothing else mattered. For a minute together or fifty years, she now had a profound understanding of the reasoning behind Romeo's actions in Shakespeare's famous work. She would follow Elena to her death, and she had, who knew how many times. This time though, she hoped they would get a long, healthy, happy life together, as all souls deserved to enjoy.

When had she become such a romantic?

The rustle of plastic broke the silence and jostled Tess from her thoughts as Elena wrapped two handmade sandwiches in cellophane—ham and turkey with guacamole, bacon, and tomato on rye. She meticulously folded them over and pressed the ends firmly together to keep them fresh. Next, she began sorting fruit from the large bowl into a smaller one for their trip.

Tess snapped into action, remembering she was responsible for the cooler. She emptied a bag of ice inside and smoothed it out, then set the container of Mai's leftover homemade potato salad securely on top. Satisfied with her work, she turned and rested against the counter. It was a good place to admire her new wife as she moved with a quiet grace about the kitchen.

Wife.

A word that had once struck fear in Tess's heart was now a source of great comfort. But saying the word was brand new to Tess. For the last few hours, she had rolled it over her tongue, adjusting to the feel and taste of it. Like the most wonderful piece of dark chocolate, she had developed an affinity quickly and craved indulgence. Especially, when coupled with the sight of the woman "wife" referred to.

A mischievous smile took shape as she continued to stare. Tanned shoulders stood out from a black tank top and tight blue jeans hugged Elena's curvy figure. The bright bird tattoo, which Tess had learned was a phoenix—how very appropriate— stared back at her.

Oh, how many times she had seen that bird, but missed the woman standing before her. And now, here they were, married of all things. Who would've thought? Her fate as a loner had been accepted long ago without complaint, until the universe, or God, or whomever, had stepped in. The missing piece that had kept

Tess from loving another had been held safe by the woman standing before her, waiting for the right moment. Now, any other way of life was unimaginable. In fact, she could hardly remember what her life had been like pre-Elena.

She didn't even want to.

"What?" Elena asked with a laugh as she placed the sandwiches alongside the potato salad. Her smile widened when Tess's answer was a wicked grin and the raking of eyes up and down her body. "Keep looking at me like that and we'll never make it to our picnic."

"It *is* our honeymoon."

"True." Elena closed the distance with a sway in her hips.

Tess stood awestruck. It wasn't the first time since they'd met and it definitely wouldn't be the last. Elena was everything she had never dated before—short hair, full-figured, confident in her own skin, independent, luminous. Elena was a brilliant star that refused to be cloaked by a cloudy night, a reminder that no one could diminish your light if you were strong enough to defy their will.

As Elena grew near, Tess was drawn into her gravity. She gripped onto soft curves to steady herself as she was pulled into a deep, sensuous kiss.

Elena licked her lips as she pulled back just enough to mumble, "Mmm. I could do that all day."

"And I would let you." Tess kissed her again, hungrily, and pulled her in flush. Her thigh slipped between Elena's in hopes of carrying their activity a bit further. She wouldn't need much.

"Maybe we can continue when we get to the river?" Elena suggested, though her body remained tightly pressed to Tess's.

A rumbling groan voiced her disappointment. Tess dropped her head but smiled anyway. She'd never say no. Besides, it was a beautiful day and there was an actual purpose to their trip. "Fine."

"You ready to make good memories?"

"I am, but you know we could make those right here too?" Tess quirked her brow and suggestively pulled her bottom lip between her teeth. Didn't hurt to ask again.

Elena laughed and untangled herself from Tess's possessive hold, then stepped back. "I do, but it won't be the same. It's the day Mary and Abigail died in this forest. Also, just a year ago, we were both in the hospital. Grandma Mai is right. We need to change the karma of this date so it doesn't haunt us in another lifetime too."

"I can't believe I'm saying this, but I agree." Agreed with the plan, but not with Elena standing so far away. Okay, so it was only a step, but it was farther than Tess had wanted. Staying in and continuing their naked celebration was her preferred option.

"You're so sexy when you agree with me." Deep brown eyes sparkled as Elena leaned back in and gave her a chaste peck on the lips. She lingered, her lips a mere half-inch away, creating a cold, empty space between them. They may as well have been miles apart.

The heat dissipated and Tess fluttered helplessly like a dying leaf in the fall breeze. She longed for the return of the warmth—not only provided by the soft caress of Elena's lips, but also the heat it generated in the farthest reaches of her body.

"But not quite as sexy as you are in those hiking boots and cargo shorts," Elena added, emphasized by a naughty wiggle of her brows.

"Oh really?" Noted for future reference. "No one else ever liked them," Tess pouted, followed by a laugh that brought a wry smile to her wife's inviting lips. Her eyes darted down as Elena moistened them, providing a spark to the withering flame within. Elena was so damned kissable. No intervention in the world could rid Tess of the addiction.

"Hmm. Their loss." Elena shrugged, then hummed and looked to the ceiling. Her lips pursed and quirked to the left, a look Tess had learned meant she was lost in deep thought. A brief moment later, Elena's gaze locked with Tess's as she spoke in a low, sexy growl, "But nothing compares to you in a black suit with those black and white wingtips."

Tess's knees nearly buckled. "Is that so?" she croaked out.

"Definitely," Elena stated without a hint of waver. She nodded for reinforcement.

Tess grabbed a hold of Elena's hand and pulled her back against her body, not only to regain the contact she had missed, but also to steady herself. The flame roared to life again. "Like the time you saw me in the hotel hallway?" Her arms encircled Elena's waist, keeping her pressed close to prevent escape, not that there was any attempt. Maybe there was hope for a quickie after all.

"Mhm." Elena followed suit, claiming Tess as her own willing captive. "It was so bizarre when you came down the stairs for our dinner date in Atlanta wearing that same suit and those shoes..." she trailed off in memory, before returning to the present to add, "then, it was like BAM! Holy shit! That was Ms. Seattle Marriott!"

Her wife's laugh was infectious. "But if I remember correctly, it didn't hit you until you saw me from behind. Why was that again?" asked Tess with a twinkle in her eye.

"Because you have an unforgettable ass." Elena burst out laughing and buried her face in Tess's chest. "I still wonder," she started, her words partially muffled, "how many other times I may have seen you and didn't know it? There were a couple of weird instances."

Tess's love for Elena had grown with each day and her own memory of that "aha moment" came to life. "I remember when I first saw your tattoo. It was through a window in Kansas City. For some reason, I had to meet the woman with the bright bird tattoo. I dragged my friend inside with me, but you were gone. It was the worst feeling and I had no idea why. There was a fleeting glimpse again as I drove away in Seattle.

"At the time, I didn't realize it was the same tattoo. Then, when I found you in Portland, it was that bird, the phoenix, that caught my attention. At first, it was a vague familiarity, then it hit me that it had been the same one. That's when you turned around."

Elena tipped her head up to meet Tess's eyes and smiled in a way that made every nerve ending fire like a New Year's Eve firework show. Goosebumps. Giddiness. Pulse pounding joy. Unconditional love. So many feelings and Tess was addicted to each and every one. The internal bonfire that heated her from head to toe was a pretty great feeling too.

"When I saw your face and those brown eyes," an expression of awe took over as Tess pulled from her memory banks, "I swear my heart skipped three beats. I couldn't even breathe." She tightened her embrace. "You'd been so close to me at least twice before, but I had missed you. I recalled each one so vividly. The voice leading me to you had been quite the eye opener, and the feelings that flowed through me when I finally stood before you were unmistakable, but that moment of recognition sealed my belief that we were meant to be together. The dreams, the voice, it all made sense. The universe wouldn't take no for an answer."

"What an interesting journey, huh?"

"Yeah, but I'm more interested in what's to come than how we got here. It's sure to be a much better ride." Tess trailed down

Elena's jawline with a peppering of kisses that brought an approving hum from her wife.

"Then, we should start with a clean slate."

Tess froze mid-kiss at the spot between Elena's clavicle and neck. Did she hear right? No. Couldn't be. She was just getting started. Determined to press the issue, her fingers dug hard into denim clad hips, then slid downward. As she palmed Elena's round cheeks, she begged, "But...can't we-"

Elena kissed her hard and fast, then made an escape with more stealth than Cat Woman could ever dream. "You take the cooler and I'll grab our mystery box."

Like a bucket of water on a candle, the flame had been extinguished. Tess rolled her eyes. "I always get the heavy lifting." A pout punctuated Tess's complaint, which earned her a playful swat on the rear.

"Gotta keep that ass in shape." Elena chuckled as she walked away, once again adding a delicious sway to her hips.

Tess took the time to enjoy the show until Elena disappeared into the bedroom. The little display did nothing to curb Tess's idea of ditching the picnic. Only an iron will brought about by her wife's deep desire to right the wrongs of a past life kept her from storming in, dragging her back to bed, and having her way with her. Surely, Elena would give in when she nibbled that spot right between her-

"I thought you were getting the cooler, hon." Humor laced her words as Elena peeked out of the bedroom.

Damn! Almost to the good part too.

A smile spread ear to ear and lit Elena's eyes. Like a sixth sense, she always seemed to know when Tess was daydreaming about sex.

"If that is truly your wish, my love?" Tess asked. The answer was a given, but could it really hurt to ask one last time?

"Oh, I have several wishes you could grant this week, but today, that's the one."

Heat rose low in Tess's belly as her imagination ran wild with possibilities. "I am at your service," she replied and obediently picked up the cooler. It was heavier than she'd thought, causing her biceps to flex and her core to tighten. "She really *is* trying to keep my ass in shape," she mumbled to herself through a chuckle as she carried it outside.

"Thank you. Be right out."

A heavy breath burst from Tess's chest as she set the cooler in the back of the Wrangler beside a bag with a blanket and silverware. She opened the top and found the source of the unexpected extra weight—a bottle of Moët and Chandon Nectar Imperial Rose champagne. Just like the one at their wedding.

"Sneaky wife." She smiled. "When'd she put that in?"

Just then, Elena strode from the cabin with a backward-facing blue ball cap. At first, Tess's eyes did as they had every day since she'd found her soulmate. They soaked up every detail, every delicate movement, and the sexy, knowing grin Elena sported as she made her approach. Then, they drifted to the medium-sized, rectangular, navy blue box under her arm with a white bow on top.

The box had awaited them at their secluded, informal wedding venue at the falls. No sender was noted, only a message saying it was not to be opened until their honeymoon. No one at the wedding had claimed responsibility for its arrival and while they had both admitted to being "creeped out," as Elena had put it, there was also something about it that had called to them.

Where she once may have left such an odd item at the venue, or even called in the bomb squad to examine it, so many unexplainable things had already happened. What was one more, right?

When Elena reached Tess, she pulled the box from under her arm and presented their mystery gift on her palms as if held on a platter. Their eyes met for a breath, then turned back to the box. They stared at it for the umpteenth time. What contents did it hold?

The wait would soon end.

∞ ∞ ∞

A sizzle of energy teased Elena's skin the moment they set foot on the rocky path of Deep Creek Loop that would lead them riverside. The hairs on her arm stood erect, but it wasn't in response to fear. No, it was comfortable, like coming home after a trip to Grandma Mai's warm hug and Chloe racing to the door for a snuggle. When they had planned their special day, both of them had looked at the map of Smoky Mountain National Park and simultaneously pointed to this trail. Neither could explain the instinct, but both had agreed it would be silly to argue with the fates. After all, they had brought them together.

They followed the path until Elena pulled them to a stop beside a slightly worn deer trail. Not much foot traffic had traveled through, yet it called to her. Her eyes met Tess's bright blues for approval. Tess nodded and then followed behind with cooler in hand as they deviated from the main walkway. The peaceful sound of water over rock grew nearer with every step until the river was in sight.

"Here," Elena said. She set the box and bag down. A gust of wind forced her to steady herself and threatened to steal her hat. She secured it to her head and looked over to Tess, who had set the cooler down and was now corralling her long dark hair into a ponytail. "You feel that?"

"Yeah. It's invigorating."

"It really is."

"I could do with a little less gust though," Tess remarked with a half-grin tugging at one corner of her mouth. Her hands settled onto her hips as she glanced around.

Elena laughed. Steady breezes did seem to accompany these experiences and she chalked it up to the spirits making themselves known. "Thank you," Elena spoke to the wind, her head tipped up to the sky.

"Who are you talking to?"

"Whomever is responsible for all of this." Elena spread her arms wide and spun around. "This magical miracle." A radiant smile was directed at her wife before she made another round. "Thank you," she said, her voice ringing louder so it carried throughout the forest.

The wind sent another heady gust that knocked her hat free. The medium-length dark strands that had been neatly pushed back under cover, were now strewn across her eyes. Leaves tumbled like ragdolls across the ground. One helpless victim ended up plastered to the side of her leg. Satisfied with its disruption, the wind fell still, releasing its hold on the poor leaf and allowing it to settle on the forest floor.

Undeterred by nature's display, Elena called out again, "Thank you for bringing us back together." She reached for Tess's hand. When it was accepted, she pulled her wife against her body and wrapped her arms around her back. The rippling of water replaced the whisper of trees and peace embraced them.

Resting her head on Tess's shoulder, she released a content sigh. "I still can't believe this is all real. The day we found one another, it was as if I'd known you my entire life, and spending the entire day talking and carrying on like old friends had been odd, but perfect."

"I know. Weird, yet oh so right." Tess's hand slid up to sift her fingers through Elena's windblown hair.

"And that night..." Elena trailed off as her memory whisked her back.

"Magical," Tess whispered, still filled with a sense of awe regarding their first time.

"Yes. Very much so." Elena stared into her eyes, then collected herself and added, "What a day it was. And boy, the look on Marlie's face when she saw you was priceless." She laughed. "Wish I had a photo. I'll have to paint that one day."

"She probably looked like I did when I met you."

"No, nothing alike. Marlie was utter disbelief, but you...you oozed love."

Pink tinged Tess's cheeks at the memory. She angled her head to look at Elena as she said, "All these years you held my heart and I never knew it. I never understood why I had never loved anyone, never wanted anyone that way, and I sure as hell never imagined getting married."

"You were waiting for me." Her fingers curled into Tess's shirt. "And I'd been searching for you all my life. You were literally the woman of my dreams."

"Sorry for the wait. Guess I should have been hit by a truck sooner."

"Thank goodness you're okay."

"Yeah well, I'm also lucky Evan didn't kill me when he got to Portland."

Elena laughed. "Boy was he frantic. But I understand. I would have been too."

Tess nodded in agreement. "Good thing I actually found you. After confessing the reason I went out there, he would have dragged me back and had me committed."

"That's all behind us now." Elena pressed a gentle kiss to Tess's lips, then said, "Time to focus on our future."

They shared a smile and unraveled themselves. "Let's get set up," Tess said and pulled the blanket from the bag.

In a matter of minutes, the blanket had been laid out, a spread of food set up, and two glasses of pink champagne were ready to be enjoyed. After a quick toast to their future, Elena glanced at the lone box beside their cooler and paused for a long moment before asking, "Should we open it?"

"I think it's time. What do you think it is?" Tess craned her neck side to side as she examined the box.

"No idea. Kinda cryptic the way they wrote 'Do not open until your honeymoon' on it. Maybe it's a sex toy," Elena offered. She waggled her brows and followed with a wicked laugh.

"Oh lord." Tess's eyes grew wide in horror at the suggestion. "If it is, we are *not* using it out here."

"Agreed. Okay, so here goes nothing." Elena peeled back the tape and lifted the top. Her brown eyes widened as she reached inside. "Oh my...I...I recognize this."

"What? What is it?" Tess crooked her neck to the right, trying to sneak a peek inside.

Elena carefully removed an eight-inch tall cedar carved great horned owl from the box. The reveal pulled an equally surprised gasp from Tess.

"Me too," Tess said, her expression one of awe as she angled left to take in all sides of the sculpture. "But I don't know why."

"I saw it in a dream once with Mary," Elena admitted. The corners of her mouth dipped into a frown as she shook her head and set the owl down on the blanket between them. How was it possible and where had it come from? Her mind flickered with the image of the old Indian from the dream. He couldn't still be alive though, could he? Or maybe he was a spirit guide?

"Is there a card or something?" Tess shook her from her thoughts when she snagged the box. She rummaged through the stuffing until her fingers found a small square of paper. "Ah ha!" A triumphant smile reigned as Tess thrust the note into the air.

Elena laughed and attempted to snatch it away, but Tess held it out of reach. "Nuh, uh. I'll read it."

"Well, hurry up, then."

∞ ∞ ∞

Elena was as giddy as a child as she waited with baited breath. Her brown eyes sparkled in the afternoon sun and her smile battled the galaxy's largest star in brightness, though for Tess, there was no competition.

Tess leaned over, steadying herself on one hand, and kissed her wife soundly, then sat back on her haunches. She'd much rather remain focused on her wife, with her flushed cheeks and deep brown eyes that blazed with the fire of desire. It was their honeymoon after all. Unfortunately, she was every bit as curious about the mysterious owl.

"Any day now," Elena blurted, breaking Tess from her musing.

"All right, hold your horses," she answered as she slowly unfolded the note. Her brow furrowed as she skimmed the words. "Hmm."

"You. Are. Killing. Me. Tess," Elena whined with a huff.

Tess laughed and nudged her gently. "Sorry. Jeeze."

"What does it say?"

"May the Great Spirit walk with you always."

"Sounds like something Grandma Mai would write." Elena's face scrunched in deep thought. "I've heard that before though. Who's it from?"

Shaking her head, Tess said, "It's not signed."

"Does it say anything else?"

It did, but Tess didn't answer. She couldn't. What did it all mean?

"Tess, honey…" Elena slowly extracted the paper from Tess's frozen fingers and scanned it for herself.

Elizabeth Smith & Anne Williams 1715-1729

Maria Hampton & Rose Davis 1869 - 1894

Abigail Carter & Mary McGhee 1945 - 1954

Contessa Kenner & Elena Jake 2017 -

"What do you think it means?"

Tess remained speechless, rolling over explanations in her mind. Only one made sense.

Unlike her, Elena thought out loud. "Is this us?" She continued to stare at the names and dates.

"I…I don't know. I think so," Tess replied with a shrug. Her gaze drifted to the distant tree line. "I mean, we have memories of Abigail and Mary, right? Could it be we've done this more than once before?"

"I guess. Grandma Mai would definitely say yes. Many believe in reincarnation or that some souls always travel together." She glanced up at Tess and then back to the paper. "We seem quite determined to be lesbians," she commented and then followed with a throaty laugh. "I wonder how many had happy endings?"

Unable to do anything but laugh along at the observation, Tess shook her head and pondered a question of her own. "And I wonder how many times I had to have an accident to make it happen?" She countered with an amused grin.

Elena nudged her and then laughed again. "Probably each and every time. You're so damned stubborn."

"I'm sure some things never change. Just like my love for you." The blush that spread across Elena's cheeks made Tess's heart thump a bit faster. *So beautiful.*

Clearing her throat, Elena asked, "Do you think there were more times when we didn't find one another?" She took Tess's left hand in hers and fiddled with the wedding ring newly adorning her finger.

Tess laced her fingers with her wife's and brought their joined hands to her lips. Placing a soft kiss to the back of Elena's hand, she smiled, feeling truly whole for the first time in her life. "Who knows, but it brings me a sense of peace knowing our time together doesn't have to end in this life." She looked to the cedar carved owl resting beside them, chuckling lightly when Elena stroked its head like a puppy.

"Ten lifetimes and then ten more after that." Elena spoke with conviction, still petting the owl. A light gust of wind rustled their hair and gave the trees a voice in the tone of a soft, supportive whisper.

Tess glanced around, accepting nature's words of encouragement. Never one to have believed in the mystical before, Tess was all in now. Whatever the powers at work, they would meet again after this life. "Even that wouldn't be enough."

"Never." Their eyes met and held. A comfortable silence filled the air, but all that was needed was the fullness in her heart.

Overwhelmed by the moment, Elena broke away and turned to set the owl at the edge of the blanket. "What number do you think this is? I mean, do you think there's been more than what's on that paper?" she asked and slid over until they were sitting hip to hip.

"Whatever one it is, I'm just happy we have today."

"Same here." Elena placed a tender kiss on Tess's cheek.

Tess turned to meet her smiling eyes. She nudged Elena to lay down and then settled in alongside, intertwining their hands once again. Staring up at the tops of green trees piercing the clear blue sky, Tess let out a satisfied sigh and squeezed her hand. "I do know I'll cherish each and every lifetime with you."

"Me too."

THE END

ABOUT THE AUTHOR

S.W. Andersen writes sapphic romances for those who believe love knows no boundaries. She has written five novels, including two Amazon best-selling lesbian romances. Having been raised by her mother, a strong female character in her own right, she has always been attracted to stories that depict independent, capable, determined women. While life tends to surround us with negativity, she prefers to fill it with happily ever afters.

S.W. has spent a large part of her life around horses and rodeos and has always had an affinity for the cowgirl lifestyle. Her love of the mountains and westerns were the driving forces behind her Sarah Sawyer western series. When she isn't working, she enjoys outdoors activities and traveling with her wife, Dianna. They share their ten acres in rural Florida with a rambunctious crew of two dogs, four cats and two horses.

swandersenwrites.com

www.ingramcontent.com/pod-product-compliance
Lightning Source LLC
Chambersburg PA
CBHW030235200626
46816CB00002BA/378